The Cowboy and His Runaway

Rock Spings Texas - Book 1

Kaci M. Rose

Five Little Roses Publishing

Book Cover By: **Sarah Kil Creative Studio**

Editing By: Anna @ Indie Hub

Blurb

A protective cowboy, a girl on the run, and crash landing that shakes them both.

No cowboy ever expects to find a woman hiding in their barn.

Much less one that is a beautiful as Riley, even with the bruises.

I vow to protect her, from whatever she is running from.

I will protect her from everything... everything but me.

Tigger Warning:

This book features a strong sassy heroine pulling herself by her bootstraps out of an abusive relationship. She gets her revenge but if this situation is a trigger for you be warned.

To the coffee that keeps me going and the kids
that call me Mommy.

Contents

Get Free Books!

Would you like some free cowboy books?
If you join Kaci Rose's Newsletter you get books free!
Join Kaci M. Rose's newsletter and get your free books!
Now on to the story!

Read the Audiobook!

This book is also available in audio! Get your copy to listen to as your read.
Get The Cowboy and His Runaway in Audio
https://www.kacirose.com/RunawayAudio

Prologue 1

Blaze

Thirteen Years Ago, Sage's Adoption Day

Today, my best friend has become my sister legally. It's the first time I feel like I can breathe. She's safe, no one can take her from us, and her piece of shit sperm donor is behind bars. She has been living with us for over a year now, but the adoption is legal just days after her twelfth birthday.

My parents have planned a family photoshoot on the ranch when we get home, so we have official family pictures with her in them. We're a family of six now. Jason, Megan, Sage, and myself. Colton is there too since he spends more time with our family than he does his own.

Sage wants to celebrate down by the swimming hole, so we all head out there after the photoshoot. Colton will spend the weekend with us, which isn't uncommon. He and Sage have shared a lot of the same home life, but Colton's was only bad when his dad showed up.

I'm watching Sage as she helps Mom prepare food for our dinner that we're taking down to the swimming hole on the east side of the ranch. She loves the ranch as much as I do. For the last year, I've watched Sage come out of her shell.

We've talked about running the ranch together after we get out of school. Granted, it would normally be handed down to Jason, the oldest son, but while he loves the land and pitches in to help wherever he's needed, it isn't his passion like it is mine.

Dad knows this, so he never pushes him. Sage loves the land as much as I do. I still remember how scared she was to bring up the idea of us working it together, but I hadn't even pictured it any other way.

Since she moved in, she's taken to helping Mom with the cooking. We not only cook for the six of us—seven if Colton joins in—but we cook for all the ranch hands that live on the property too. On any given night, we could have fifteen to twenty people in and out grabbing food.

Now we've loaded up into two trucks and are heading out to the swimming hole. Jason and Megan ride with Dad. Sage, Colton, and I ride with Mom.

Sage and Colton are in the backseat when Colt speaks up. "So, how does it feel to be all official?"

"Honestly, it doesn't feel much different, other than the tension is finally gone. No one can come and take me away anymore," Sage says.

I look over my shoulder at her and see her put her hand on Colt's shoulder. She knows he struggles with his dad and the tension he can pop back into his life at any time.

"I was thinking the same thing earlier today. It's like the nightmare of the last few years has ended at last. The book ends with, 'And they lived happily ever after.'" I smile.

She laughs, but I also see a hint of sadness in Mom's eyes. She didn't know what went on with Sage at first. She and I hid it well, and I only did because Sage begged me. Her dad was an abusive drunk.

I knew he was mean and loud, but I didn't know he was physical until I came home from school and asked her to go ride horses with me. I'd found her in the barn crying with some nasty bruises.

It went against every fiber in my being not to tell my parents. Sage was terrified of ending up a foster kid and being taken away from me and my family. We devised a plan that at midnight on the day she turned eighteen, we'd sneak out and run away to somewhere her sperm donor would never find her.

On the nights he came home shit drunk after he passed out, she would steal money from his wallet. Now, don't judge her. Neither of us were old enough to get a legal job yet. She would hide the money for us to use when we finally picked up and ran. He owed her that much.

She learned how to work the system—when to stay out of his way, and how to fly under the radar. Things seemed okay for a while until I found her in the barn again.

This time, Colt was with me. I'd never seen him so panicked. He learned the truth that day and we also found out he knew what she was dealing with, because his dad was the same way, only he had the decency to disappear for a year or so at a time.

The three of us bonded fast. Then a year ago, I was walking her home one night, and we could hear her dad on a rampage from outside the house. I saw the panic in her eyes, and she begged me not to make her go home.

We hid in the trees between her house and mine, and I held her, trying to calm her down. She was shaking. I knew at this point I couldn't send her back. I took her back to my house and put her on the couch in the den. She begged me not to tell my parents and to wake her before anyone woke up, so she could sneak home.

To this day, she doesn't know I went right to my parents' room and spilled everything. I cried myself to sleep that night. My parents agreed to allow her to believe they didn't know. This happened for a few weeks until Mom was up one night when my sister was sick and Sage came face to face with her. Mom had never seen Sage so scared. I told her I had and it broke Mom's heart.

That day, Mom went to talk to her parents and tried to get them to sign over guardianship to her in exchange for her silence on the matter. Seeing as Sage's sperm donor saw her as free labor, he didn't agree.

When Sage got home that day, he was already drunk and she received the worst beating she ever had. I found her, but it took both Colt and me to get her back to my house. She wouldn't talk about it, but Mom called the cops.

The sheriff was a family friend, so I could stay by her side. After photos were taken and a trip to the ER for x-rays, I had to tell everything I knew. It took a while before Sage would talk about what happened that day; she cried through it all. It broke all of our hearts.

Since Rock Springs is such a small town, it was easy to get guardianship transferred to my parents. That weekend, Mom and Megan decorated her room for her. It was right next to mine since Mom figured it would be a comfort for her.

The trial made her live it all over again, causing her nightmares. Every night. She was in therapy, but it wasn't helping. We hoped now that the adoption was done, they would start to go away.

When we reach the swimming hole, we all pile out. My parents set up seating and a food area and us kids head up the hill to the cliff and jump in. It's tradition, after all!

Jason and Megan are the first ones to jump. Colt waits for us but jumps before we make it all the way to the top. I look over and see Sage lost in thought.

"Penny for your thoughts?" I nudge her with my shoulder.

"I worry about Colt. When he heads home, he always looks terrified like he's waiting for the other shoe to drop," she says.

"I know but until his dad shows up again, we can't do much of anything. We have no proof."

"That's no way to live." She shakes her head.

I take a deep breath and check over the edge to make sure everyone is out of our way. I grab her hand and say, "I know, but all we can do is be there for him. Now let's jump."

She looks at me, smiles, and squeezes my hand. "On three."

I count to three, and we run to the edge and jump in, our hands never letting go until we hit the water. We spend the next hour laughing and swimming.

As we sit on the tailgate and eat with everyone, Sage shocks the hell out of me.

"So, I want to buy my family's ranch," she says out of the blue.

Everyone is silent, just looking at her.

"Think about it," she says. "With him in jail, my egg donor can't keep it going for long, five years at most. My sad excuse of a bio brother doesn't want it, and he has been taken from their custody, anyway. It will go up for sale, eventually."

"I thought we were gonna run this ranch together," I say.

"We ARE," she says.

Well, color me confused. And from the looks on everyone's faces, they are as well.

"We save up and buy the ranch, then we run both. We combine the two ranches and with 580,000 acres, we become the second biggest in the state overnight. I've been thinking about this. We can remodel the main house so it looks brand new and figure out who will live there. The entire place will need an overhaul by then, I'm sure. I know we can do this!"

She looks at me with a spark in her eyes. I open my mouth to speak, but she keeps going.

"My grandparents were amazing people, and that should be my land by birthright. I got shitty parents but I don't want to see what my grandparents worked so hard for vanish."

I look around and see it in my parents' eyes.

Well, okay. Game on.

By the time we head back to the house, we have a game plan. Since we have next to no debt on the ranch, we can start saving money. Jason agrees to get a job as soon as he can after school next year and put money aside. Dad will open a savings account, and we'll all add money as we can.

Dad puts a call into his buddy who runs the real estate office in town and tells him to give him a head's up when that ranch gets ready to hit the market, but he doesn't want anyone to know he's interested. He knows he can trust the guy because they grew up together.

Things are looking up. I am lying in bed that night thinking our plans over, too excited to sleep when I hear Sage having another one of her nightmares. I head into her room, followed by Colt since he's staying in the room across the hall from her.

I tell him to get Mom and Dad while I try to wake her. I finally get her to wake up as Mom comes in.

Sage is sweating and dazed soon as she realizes where she is and sees me. She clings to me for dear life. I wrap my arms around her as she cries. Mom sits beside her and rubs her back, speaking softly.

"Everything is okay, Sage. You're safe."

I can see the pain in Mom's eyes, and I can tell she sees the panic in mine. This nightmare seems worse than the others. She has never been this shaken. Colt sits behind me and rubs her arms that are wrapped around my neck.

I don't hear Dad enter the room or Megan and Jason until I hear Dad telling Megan everything is okay. He asks Jason to help Megan back to bed. They know the basics of what happened.

Jason gets it more than Megan, but we've tried to shield her. She's too innocent to be dragged into all the details.

Sage's face is buried in my chest still, but the crying has stopped. Dad suggests Colt head back to bed. When Colt gets up to leave, he comes around and hugs Sage and kisses the top of her head.

"Everything will be okay. I'm right across the hall if you need me," Colt says.

She barely nods her head while still hiding against my chest.

I make a move to shift, thinking she'll head back to sleep when she grabs onto me.

"No, Blaze, don't leave me alone," she says, panicked.

I look at Mom with no clue what to do.

"Blaze, why don't you lie down with her until she can fall back asleep," Mom says. Dad nods in agreement.

"Okay," I agree and feel Sage relax a bit.

I hug Dad who says, "You be a gentleman, or I'll kick your ass, but you seem to calm her.

She needs that."

"I promise, Dad," I say. He heads back to his room.

Then I hug Mom. "Take care of her. I'm glad she feels safe with you," she says. Then she puts her hands on my cheeks and glares at me. "No funny business, do you hear me?" She gives me her Mom voice, the one no one dares disobey.

"Mommm, I promise," I reply.

She glares at me a moment more, then nods and heads back to her room. I climb into bed and face Sage. She reaches out and holds my hand.

Don't doubt for one moment the next day I am given a three-hour birds and bees talk from Mom and a two-hour version from Dad.

"Thank you for staying," Sage says.

"Do you want to talk about it?" I ask her.

She's quiet and for a moment, I think she might have fallen asleep. Then she whispers, "They're getting more and more vivid. To the point, I have a hard time realizing it's a dream the next day. Most nights, it's just a replay of one of the times that led to you finding me in the barn. Tonight, it wasn't a memory. It was a whole new incident, and I didn't know what would happen next. That's what was the most terrifying."

"I'm right here. No one can hurt you anymore. I won't let them," I promise her.

She snuggles to my side and falls asleep. I too fall asleep into what is to become our new normal.

Prologue 2

Blaze

Seven Years Ago, Graduation Day

I wake up to my alarm, trying to figure out why I set it. Then I realize—it's graduation day. Sage, Colt, and I are graduating today. I look over, expecting Sage to be next to me. But find she isn't. I sit up. In the last six years since her adoption, her nightmares haven't stopped.

She's seen a few different therapists and has tried sleep medication, which just makes it worse. She makes us promise never to put her on medication again. The only thing that keeps the nightmares away is to sleep next to me.

There's nothing romantic, we tried kissing once, and yeah, nothing. She's my sister, my best friend, and the most important person in the world to me.

Colt has also officially been adopted into the family after his dad showed up again. He walked in on his dad beating the crap out of his mom. He tried to stop him, and his dad turned on him. Sage walked in after realizing his dad was home.

Long story short, his dad is dead, and his mom died of injuries inflicted by his dad. Colt and Sage are safe.

My parents didn't hesitate to take him in. We've also added Mac to the family. His name is Makya, which means eagle hunter, but everyone calls him Mac. Sage noticed the signs of abuse, and that whole story ended with Sage being an idiot and getting herself shot, by putting herself in harm's way, *again*, to save Mac. She gave us all quite a scare but pulled through with flying colors.

With Mac's dad now dead, he also needs a place to live. He's from the local Indian reservation and didn't have anyone who could take him in. My parents went to the tribe elders and offered him a home.

They agreed so long as we make every effort to keep his heritage alive and allow him to come to the reservation often to learn. Of course, we agreed.

The six of us kids have bonded and become fast friends. Megan never likes to hang out with us guys as much as Sage. Megan is a girly girl, and we always try to keep her sheltered from what happened with Sage, Colt, and Mac. She'll be mad if she finds out, but we aren't budging.

Since her friends started to form crushes on us guys and tried to use Megan to get to us, she stopped bringing her friends home and started going to their houses instead, so we have seen a lot less of her than before.

Our plan to buy Sage's family ranch is in full swing. Jason has been working his butt off at the bar and is set to bartend next year when he turns twenty-one. Sage has started to train horses on the side, and every penny she makes from that goes into the family savings account. Megan even adds money from her babysitting jobs.

Colt has picked up odd jobs after school in the winter when the ranch work is light. He loves the ranch as much as Sage and I, and the three of us plan to work it and learn together. Colt has had jobs from flipping burgers at the café to helping with clean up at the bar, and every penny has been added to the savings.

I've been focused on the ranch. Dad has put me in charge of the hay hauling in the fall, and I've gathered enough that we have extra to sell, making it my contribution to the fund. Mac loves the plan too. He has made it known that once he turns sixteen in a few months, he plans to do odd jobs in town.

The land hasn't gone up for sale yet, but we have more than we need for a down payment. We plan to put as much money down, so we have as little debt as possible. We'll need money to fix it up too. Sage and I check that fence line often and talk to the foreman over there when we see him in town. They're trying to live off the money the ranch makes while doing as little as possible.

This is fine by us; we'll be able to get it even cheaper. From talking to him, the ranch can only go another two or three years before they have to put it up for sale, and another four to five years before the bank takes it. They haven't been smart with the money since Sage's sperm donor went to jail.

I head down the hall to Sage's room and peek in. She's snuggled up against Colt. Since starting high school, I've joined the football team. Colt stays with her when I don't make it home in time. I notice Colt is wide awake.

I step in and lean against the door frame. "I didn't want to wake her until I had to. She was tossing and turning all night."

I sigh. I wish I knew how to help her. If all we can do is be there for her at night, that's what we'll do. Colt has been great at helping. I think he doesn't want to be alone after everything that has happened with his mom and dad.

For a while, the three of us would stay up in one of our beds watching movies until we all passed out.

Mac would join the party from time to time, though he hasn't had constant nightmares. Every now and then, he has a bad night and just doesn't want to spend it alone. I love that we've all been able to rally around and help our new siblings.

We aren't just brothers and sisters because of my parents; these are my best friends, and I know they feel the same way.

I rub Sage's arm to wake her. To say she isn't a morning person is an understatement. She wakes up grumbling something about annoying brothers.

"Sage, it's graduation day. I smell Mom cooking breakfast downstairs. We have to get moving."

That seems to spark her awake. She sits up and runs her hands through her hair. She looks over and sees Colt, and her eyes soften. I see something I can't quite place on her face as she gets out of bed.

"Thank you, Colt. Let's get ready. I can't believe we're graduating today," she says and runs downstairs for some coffee.

• • • • • • • • • •

As we head back to the house from graduation, we're all quiet. Mom and Dad ride separately from Colt, Sage, and me. We're planning what we're doing this weekend. It's kind of scary when you no longer have the safety net of school.

We all have plans to take business classes online while we work the ranch instead of going away to school. There's nothing like the hands-on learning of the ranch.

As we pull up and get out of the car, Sage speaks up. "Hey Blaze, will you take a walk with me before we head in?"

Colt looks at her for a minute and then heads inside.

We head off to the tree line to the side of the house with no destination in mind. I wait for her to talk.

"So, remember that money I'd been stealing from my sperm donor when he got drunk?"

"The money we were going to use to run away with?" I ask. I haven't thought about that plan for a long time.

"So, I'm going to do it."

"What?" I ask, clearly confused.

"Well, not run away, but I need to get out of here for a bit, Blaze. I want to travel some, and there's more than enough money to travel for a bit."

"What?" I ask again. "What about the ranch and school and the family?"

"I talked to Mom and Dad and asked them not to say anything to anyone. They get it. There's a lot of bad memories here, Blaze."

"There are a lot of good ones too."

"There are, but I need time. I need to prove I can stand on my own two feet, and I need to just breathe. Go somewhere where I'm not *that* girl, where I don't get the stares and pity looks. Yes, I STILL get them. I see it in their eyes when I'm in town. I need a break. I need to *not* be that girl."

"What about the ranch?"

"You and Colt more than have it covered. Mac wants to learn more too. You guys will be fine."

"That's not what I meant."

"Blaze, I promise if my land comes up for sale, I'll drive all night to get back here. I'm not giving up that dream, and I'm not giving up the dream of us running this place together either.

I'll still take classes online, and I won't be gone more than a year, but I do need to do it before we expand, or I'll never get the chance."

We walk for a while in silence while I take it all in. I feel like she's running. I get the bad memories, but her whole support system is here.

"What are you running from?" I ask her. We have never had any secrets between us, and we've always been blunt.

I see the surprise in her face before she answers, "Everything, and nothing at the same time."

"When are you leaving?"

"Tomorrow sometime. Need to make the last plans."

"Where are you going?"

"I want to see the National Parks, put my feet in the Pacific and the Atlantic Oceans, see the Northern Lights, and swim with dolphins. I'm going to see where life takes me. I plan to pick up odd jobs, and I'll be back in a year, or when the money runs out, or if the land goes up for sale.

I know it sounds flaky, and I know I don't have a real plan, but I need to do this. I promise to stay in touch and maybe you can fly out and spend a weekend with me. We always talked about going to the Grand Canyon together. I'd still like to do that."

I sigh. How can I tell this girl no? After everything she has been through. I won't lie, her being out there alone terrifies me, but I get why she needs to do this.

"I'd really like to explore the Grand Canyon with you. Just not during hell week, okay?"

"Okay." She smiles at me.

I stare straight ahead. "You swear you'll come back?" I ask her.

"I swear I will. This isn't forever."

I stop and hug her as tight as I possibly can. "Promise you'll call a few times a week, if not every day. I want to hear every detail of your travels. I mean every detail. Make me feel like I'm there with you."

She giggles against my chest. "I promise, Blaze."

We turn to slowly head back to the house.

"Blaze, don't say anything to anyone until tomorrow. I want to take my time telling everyone myself. Please, Blaze," she pleads.

"Of course, I won't say anything."

"Thank you." She links her arm through mine, and we head back to the house for our graduation party.

• • • • • • • • • •

Later that night, I come into her room. She's on her computer, and I assume is making some last-minute plans. She sees me and smiles.

"Hey, I have some things to do. I plan to be up late. Is it okay if I just lie down with you later tonight when I'm done?" she asks.

"Of course. I'm beat. I'll probably fall asleep fast."

"Okay, night," she says as I head to my room.

I get ready for bed and then lie down. I'm thinking about how different life will be without her here as I drift off to sleep.

• • • • • • • • • •

I wake up and see Sage isn't next to me. I get up and head to her room, and it looks like she's packed. She must be planning to head out early.

I head downstairs for breakfast and see Mom and Dad sitting at the table. Their heads are bent down, whispering.

"Mornin'," I say, yawning as I head over to pour my coffee.

"Did you know?" Mom asks.

"Know what?"

"That Sage was planning to leave in the middle of the night and not give anyone the chance to say goodbye?"

A bit of panic floods through me. "No, she said she was leaving today."

Mom stands and hands me a letter. "We found this on the counter this morning."

Hey Everyone,

I am horrible with goodbyes, and I couldn't stand to see anyone cry. I need to get away from here for a bit and get away from all the memories here. I promise this isn't forever. This is just for a little bit.

Don't worry, I'll be fine, and I promise to check in. Regularly.

Blaze, I promise I'll share every detail. I won't forget.

Jason, you better be running that bar by the time I get back!

Megan, finish school, and I promise to be back for your graduation.

Mac, stay strong and if you need me, call me, any time of day.

Colt, I'm sorry.

I love you guys and will miss you like crazy.

- Sage

To say I'm shocked is an understatement. I'm unprepared for her to leave, much less for her to sneak off in the middle of the night.

As I'm processing all this, Colt comes downstairs. I barely hear Mom telling him what's going on, then taking the letter from me and handing it to him.

I look over at him and wonder why it looks like his whole world just ended.

Chapter 1

Blaze

Current Day

I'm woken by Colt staggering into his room next to mine. I glance up at the clock. It's two a.m. Nothing new. Colt has gained a reputation as a bit of a playboy. He's tamed quite a bit since his worst following high school, but when he goes out, this is normal. He never brings a girl home. Sage's rules and all, but he doesn't go out as often anymore.

Sage came back for Megan's graduation just like she promised. Then she left again. Something bothered her when she left, but she wouldn't talk. A few months later, she and I headed out to the Grand Canyon. We spent a lot of time talking. Her nightmares had stopped since she'd been gone. She'd seen so many places, dated some guys, and we talked about it all. The Grand Canyon was everything we had planned and more.

On our fourth day, Dad called to say Sage's family ranch was getting ready to go on the market. True to her promise, Sage came back and dived into ranch life headfirst. I could tell she needed the time away; she had been through a lot, and she deserved it.

When the ranch went up for sale, we were able to put in an anonymous full-price bid, and they accepted. When they realized it was us on closing day, they tried to back out, but they were obligated by law at that point, and we bought the property.

Sage had said she did a lot of thinking while she was away, and she wanted to renovate the main house. We had the money and did a lot of it ourselves where we could. After two years, it was done. She shocked us all when she moved into the house. She said she had to conquer and take control of the memories.

She talked to Jason, Megan, Mac, and me to move in with her. It took a lot more talking to get Colt to move in. But like me, he really couldn't deny her anything either.

So, here we are. She still has nightmares, but only when they're triggered. Maybe two to three a year now.

Dad is semi-retired now, and he works the ranch as needed. I've taken over the east side, and Sage has taken over the west side. We run them together under the same name, but we each run a separate crew and come to help each other as needed. Colt bounces between the two as needed but spends more time with my crew.

Mac is the ranch manager on Sage's side. He loves it and has said he doesn't want the headache of owning a ranch but loves working it. Jason now owns and runs the bar, and Megan owns the salon in town. Both help on the ranch as needed, but it has never been their dream.

I drift back to sleep and wake to my six-a.m. alarm. Smelling coffee and bacon is enough to get me out of bed.

I head downstairs to see Sage cooking omelets, bacon, and biscuits. I come up behind her and look over her shoulder. Her long, brown hair is pulled up in a messy bun, and she has her usual pajamas of gym shorts and a t-shirt on.

I make a cup of coffee and sit at the table to wait for her to finish breakfast.

"Did you hear Colt stumble in last night?" she asks.

"Yeah, I swear it's like he tries to wake me up when he comes home drunk like that."

Sage rolls her eyes. "Wouldn't surprise me."

As Sage finishes breakfast, everyone rolls downstairs to eat and grab a coffee.

As usual, we talk about ranch business and plans for the day.

"I'm thinking of starting a live music night at the bar," Jason says. "Bring in some local talent and sign some small tours. What do you guys think?"

"Would you keep it to country music?" Sage asks.

"Of course. Got to stay true to who we are." Jason grins.

"I like the idea. I might know someone who'd like the exposure, though I might have to do some talking since it's in a bar," Sage says.

"You always know someone for everything," Colt says.

"I met a lot of people while I traveled, and I made it a point to keep in touch with them."

Colt grunts and gets up to put his plate in the sink and stomp out of the house like he does every time Sage mentions her travels.

She sighs. "I don't think he's forgiven me for leaving like I did."

"Have you talked to him about it?" Megan asks.

"He won't talk about it. Always seems to change the subject or have somewhere else to be. I've given up." Sage sighs, watching after where Colt stormed off.

"He's hard-headed, but he'll come around," Jason says.

"Well, I think I'm ready to take on another girl at the salon," Megan says, changing the subject. "We have the clients for it, but I'm having a hard time finding someone. If any of you know anyone who wants to work in small town USA, let me know."

After Megan has left, Mac, Sage, and I talk a bit of ranch business before Sage gets a call. One of her clients is there to drop off a horse for training, and she heads out.

I head over to the east side of the ranch to check with my crew, making a mental list of things I need to pick up in town. I see Colt heading into the barn and follow him in. "Hey, you need to talk to Sage. We can all pick up on the tension between you two when she talks about her travels."

He grunts. "I have nothing to say."

I look at him. "What is your deal? I get she didn't say goodbye the way she should have, but we've all forgiven her and moved on. You can't tell me you don't know why she did it, you understand it more than I do."

"Oh, I understand all right. Look, I don't want to talk about it. I promise to talk to Sage, but not right now, okay?"

I nod. That will have to be good enough. I don't want to push him, though I feel like there's something he isn't telling me.

For the rest of the day, I take inventory and head into town to get supplies. I need to pick up some groceries Sage has asked for and run some errands. I can't shake this feeling deep down in my gut that this is the calm before the storm.

I've had this feeling a few times in my life, normally right before I'd find Sage hiding in the barn. I felt it again right before Colt's dad showed up for the last time, and again the night before everything happened with Mac.

It's a feeling I hate, one that scares the crap out of me because I know something is coming, but I have no idea from where.

Heading to bed that night, I try to place all my ducks in a row. I check on Sage and browse the court files, making sure her sperm donor is still in jail. I fall asleep with my gun by my bed and my hand on my phone, praying I'm just overreacting.

Chapter 2

Riley

My heart is racing as I tiptoe around the house. It takes forever for him to pass out this time. Between the drinks and drugs, he's getting stronger, the busted lip, double black eye, at least two broken ribs prove that much. The drugs make him different; energetic and crazy. It takes longer for him to pass out.

I don't have much of a plan; I just know I have to try. I haven't had any time to pack anything. I just take my purse and run. We live in a rundown trailer outside of town, so I run toward the interstate, away from town. Away from anyone who knows me, who knows Jed. I stay off the road and stumble along until I make it to the interstate.

I know, I know. It's stupid, but I try to hitchhike, deciding a random stranger can't be as bad as Jed. Finally, a semi-truck pulls over and while I am scared shitless, the thought of ending back up at Jed's scares me more, so I jump in.

I breathe a sigh of relief to see the trucker is a woman. She takes one look at me and can tell what I am running from. "Shit, let's get you to the ER." She panics and starts jabbing her index finger on her phone, pulling up the closest ER on her phone.

This will just lead me back to Jed.

"No, please. He'll find me that way. I'm heading to a friend's house, one he doesn't know. I'll find a doctor there. I just need to get away from here."

She watches me closely and then nods and pulls back onto the road.

"I have a delivery in a small town outside Dallas before I head north toward home," she says.

Dallas. That's four hours from here in good traffic.

"If you can stand my company that long, I'd appreciate the ride to your stop. I can call my friend from there in the morning and see if she can come get me. I didn't want to call from anywhere he could trace it before I left," I tell her.

I hate lying, but I don't think she'll let me just walk away if she knows I have no place to go.

"That's fine, honey. I just ask you to keep me company. Haulin' can get lonely, so tell me any stories ya got!"

I smile as I see signs for Houston as we head north.

We talk about places we've been, our childhood. I tell her about growing up on a ranch, and even about how my mom, dad, and brother died. While not something I've talked about recently, it's a better subject than anything Jed related.

She tells me some of her stories, places she has been, about the time she picked up a hitchhiker who had a pig shoved in her bag, and how the pig got loose and ran around the cab of her truck.

I like her, maybe in another life, we could have been friends. Lilly is her name. If I ever have kids, my daughter's name will be Lilly. This woman truly is an angel.

At about eleven a.m., we're north of Austin after having to fight traffic. Lilly says she has to pull over and rest, something about regulations. She pulls into a truck stop, and we head in to use the restroom. My stomach grumbles, and I can't remember the last time I ate.

I have about forty dollars on me, and I'm not starving enough to use it just yet. That money has to get me as far as possible. I head back to the truck, and Lilly comes back with some water and food.

"You need to eat. The sooner you can get your strength back, the sooner you can heal and put that bastard behind bars where he belongs."

I pull out my wallet and try to hand her some money for the food, but she waves me off. "I won't take your money. This is thanks for keeping me company."

"Thank you," I say as tears well up in my eyes. No one has ever been this nice to me, not since my parents died.

"Listen, my sister was in an abusive relationship. She was lucky enough to have someone help her out of it. Because of that, she's alive and home with us today. I'm paying it forward, okay?"

"Thank you. I should have had more of a plan, but I saw an opening to run and just did."

"That was so brave of you. I'm glad I was there to help."

Lilly has a little living area in the back of her cab. After some fighting, I convince her I'm fine to sleep on the floor since she has to drive and all. We sleep a good portion of the day. Lilly says she prefers to travel at night since the traffic is less.

She also says something about how her delivery has to be a nighttime one, out of business hours to some cattle café? I'm not fully listening, but what I catch doesn't make much sense.

When we wake up, we hit the bathroom again. Lilly brings back more water and food, and we head out. By now, it's after eight p.m., and the traffic is smooth until we see signs for Dallas.

As we fight Dallas traffic, Lilly says her stop is in Rock Springs. I have no phone, otherwise I'd look it up and figure out my next plan. Lilly says there's a nice diner there and even a bed and breakfast if needed until my friend can come to get me. I smile and play along.

I've never been to Dallas, but I've always heard it's big. Lilly says Dallas and Fort Worth all run together in one big city with a bunch of smaller cities mixed in. You can't tell where one starts and the other ends.

Even late at night, the traffic is crazy. It's a Friday night, so I'm guessing people are just going out, but I'm still in awe.

As we leave the city lights behind, Lilly says we still have another hour and a half. I smile and thank her again.

We continue to talk, and I'm thankful she doesn't push me about Jed, so much so I'm willing to talk and answer questions about anything else in my life.

As we get off the interstate, I notice the sign doesn't even say Rock Springs on it. When I ask Lilly, she says the town is a ways off the beaten path being so small.

Well shit, there goes my plan to hitchhike again. I can't tell her to let me off here because she'll know I'm lying about having someone to call. So, I smile and hope something works out once we get there.

As we pull into town, Lilly pulls into a feed store that's attached to a diner. We hug and say our goodbyes. I tell her I'm going to grab a room at the bed and breakfast we just passed and call my friend.

She gives me a piece of paper with her cell number on it and says to call her if I need anything. She travels this route several times a week and will be happy to help or just meet up for coffee.

I'm grateful and put her number in my wallet.

I head in the direction of the B&B, my tummy rumbling an angry growl. I see the neon signs for a bar across the street. Making sure Lilly can't see me, I head around the back, hoping I can pick up some scrap food.

What the hell has my life come to, eating scrap food from the back of a bar? I still have forty dollars. If it means I can get a bit more freedom by giving up some pride by eating the other half of some drunk's cheeseburger, then so be it.

I can't go back to Jed. I won't. I know next time he'll kill me. The more drugs he uses, the stronger he gets. When I've tried to run in the past, everyone in town just hands me back over to him like I'm his property to do with as he pleases. He even made me quit my job with the promise of going to school, just so I had no reason to go into town.

I flinch. That was the night I knew I had to find a way to run. He swore I was cheating on him with my boss. He made a huge scene and made me quit and beat me for 'cheating on him.' I wasn't, but he wouldn't believe me. My boss might have flirted with me from time to time, but I never returned it. He was married, for crying out loud.

I sigh and try to push the memory away. I can't hide out behind the bar for the rest of my life; eventually, someone will find me.

I hear the bar door open, and the music gets louder before the door closes. I hear two guys fighting and yelling. I start shaking, my body's reaction to guys yelling. I panic. I can't run. Lilly might see me. While I think of her as the closest thing I have to a friend, she can't know I lied to her.

I can't stay here; they might find me. I see a pickup truck behind the bar and jump in the bed. There are blankets in the back, so I pull them over me to hide.

I listen to them fight and argue. I hear the bar door opening and closing with more people filing out. I have no idea what time it is, but I wait for a quiet moment. Exhaustion takes over first.

· · · ● · ● · · ·

I jolt awake as the pickup truck I've been hiding in starts up.

Shit!

I'd fallen asleep. The events from the last twenty-four hours have caught up with me.

My mind races. What are my options?

There's no telling who's driving and what kind of person they are.

I have no idea what the time is or where we're going.

So, I stay where I am. I figure once he or she gets to their destination, I can get out and run down the road from there.

After a few minutes, and several turns, the road gets bumpy. I realize then just how much pain I really am in.

I feel like I got hit by a semi-truck. I guess the adrenaline has kept me going, along with the pain meds from Lilly.

Every bump makes me want to cry. After a few more turns, the bumps get worse. I want to scream in pain but know I can't.

Finally, the truck slows down and stops. A minute later, the engine shuts off, and I hear the truck door open and slam shut.

I pray the owner doesn't come to the back of the truck.

I strain to hear what sounds like a house door open and close. I wait several minutes, then uncover my head and stare up at the stars and listen. It's quiet out here. No lights, just the moon. I haven't seen stars this bright since I lived on my parents' ranch.

It hurts to breathe, but I know I can't stay here. I also know I won't make it far. I peek my head over the side of the truck. The house is dark and quiet. I look around and realize I'm on a ranch, which means the town is now who knows how far away. We had been driving for quite a bit.

I see a huge barn behind me and figure I'll take my chances there for the night. I need to rest before I can get moving again.

I almost fall trying to get out of the truck. The pain is so bad, it knocks the breath out of me.

I get to the barn. It's dark and quiet as I get inside and brace myself against the wall to catch my breath. There's a ladder leading up to the hayloft. There's a lot of hay up there. If it's anything like my parents' ranch, I'll be able to hide in some back corner behind the hay.

I can hide out for the day to rest and then make my move tomorrow night. They shouldn't be up there much this time of year.

I head to the ladder and almost blackout climbing up. The pain is unlike anything I've experienced before, each breath a short and sharp jab in the lungs. I make it... barely. I get to the back corner of the barn and don't have to maneuver the bales of hay to hide so no one will see me if they walk up.

I see a busted open bale and use it to make a makeshift bed and send up a silent prayer no one finds me right before I pass out from the pain.

Chapter 3

Blaze

The next morning, I still can't shake the feeling in my gut, but everyone is fine, so I have to be happy about that.

I watch everyone at breakfast, and they're all relaxed and have no clue how I feel.

"Hey guys, please be on extra alert today. Stay sharp and watch your backs," I say.

Sage drops her fork. I can tell she instantly knows what's wrong. We can read each other like a book. "What's up, Blaze?"

"Nothing, I hope. Just a feeling I haven't been able to shake since yesterday." My brothers and sisters are watching me. My gut has never been wrong; no one knows that better than Sage and Colt. I see the worry in both their eyes. But everyone agrees.

Colt is the first one out the door, as always. We wrap up the conversation, and Sage says she has some work to do in the office before she heads out to work with the horses. She has set up an office in the house, her dream office, she says. Complete with a fireplace, floor-to-ceiling bookcases and French doors overlooking the ranch.

I put on my boots, grab my hat, and head out to the barn to make sure they'll be okay until Sage gets out there later.

I'm lost in my own little world, thinking of the back fence we need to check this week. It's been a while since we've run fence checks. Though I won't lie, by running the back fence, I can also check up on the property behind us. The sweetest family owns it, but they have no one to hand it down to. Eventually, it will go up for sale.

Though the sale could be tomorrow or ten years from now, I've been thinking of bringing it up to the family. We should get ready to make an offer on it when it does. It would almost double our land now. I know Colt would love a space to run himself. The main house would be someplace for him to have his own space.

I know he wasn't thrilled to move in with all of us, but he also couldn't tell Sage no. She pulled the damn puppy-dog eyes and pouty lip with him, and it was over. Thankfully, she rarely pulls out the big guns like that, but when she does, you know you've lost because she'll stop at nothing to get her way then.

I'm not paying attention as I head to the barn until I see Colt right in front of me. I look up at him, and his face is pure panic. Mac walks up beside me at the same moment I realize something is very wrong.

"Mac, get Sage, now!" Colt snaps.

Mac turns and to his credit, he runs.

"Looks like your gut was right once again," Colt says as he turns and heads back to the barn. "Follow me and keep quiet."

I follow Colt, and my stomach turns. Everyone was accounted for at breakfast this morning; who the hell is it this time?

I watch Colt climb the ladder to the hayloft, and my blood runs cold. Memories of climbing this ladder and the condition we would find Sage in at the back of this very hayloft flood my mind. Instantly, I'm ten years old again, reliving the worst year of my life. For a split second, I understand Sage's nightmares better than ever.

Sage runs in as I'm about to follow Colt up the ladder, and I hold my finger to my lips to keep them quiet. I have no idea what we're about to see, but I trust Colt.

Once we all get up to the loft, we follow Colt to the back.

"I was up here tossing hay down for the stalls this morning and noticed the hay in the back wasn't the way we left it," he whispers. "I thought maybe the guys were up here messing around like we used to."

"I'm guessing that's not what it was?" Sage whispers.

"No," Colt says. One cold word lets me know what we're about to find isn't good.

Wanting to protect Sage, I step ahead of her and head over to look at what we're dealing with first. I feel like someone just sucker punched me in the gut. I can't breathe.

I see a girl lying on a bed of hay, her blond hair tied up in a messy knot at the top of her head. She's in a faded t-shirt, jeans, and sneakers. What takes my breath away are the two black eyes she sports, how pale she is, and her busted lip.

The bruises on her arms and legs are fresh. A day or two old at most. Even with all that, she's still the most beautiful girl I've ever seen.

"Shit," I say a little louder than I mean to.

The girl stirs as Sage looks over my shoulder, and I hear her suck in her breath. I instantly feel the need to protect this girl. There's a strange pull and a need to beat the shit out of the bastard who dared to lay a hand on her.

The girl opens her eyes and looks around to get her bearings, then sees us. I can only imagine what it looks like. Colt and I stand shoulder to shoulder with Mac and Sage behind us.

Once she looks over at the four of us, her eyes get as big as saucers, and I see the sheer panic in her eyes. She pulls her legs in front of her and wincing in pain, she scoots backward. "Please, no..."

Sage pushes forward and turns to glare at us, the glare that says she'll have our hides later.

What the hell did I do now?

I watch as Sage slowly walks over to the woman. "It's okay. We won't hurt you." She speaks in such a soft tone.

I go to take a step toward the girl, and Sage turns her head toward me. "Don't move," she says harshly and glares at me. "Don't you see she's terrified? The three of you are the last thing she needs right now."

In the back of my mind, I know she's right. I know this girl is probably terrified of any man in general right now, but I can't turn around and leave. I have to stay by her side and make sure she's okay.

Sage turns back to her. "My name is Sage, and they're my brothers: Blaze, Colt, and Mac." She points to each of us. She's near the girl now and lowers herself to her knees at the girl's side.

It's a move I've done with Sage when she was beaten, bruised, and scared. Instantly, I do the same. Get down on her level instead of towering over her. Try to calm her.

Sage looks over at us. "Why don't you guys keep the ranch hands out of the barn. Keep them busy elsewhere for now. Don't tell them anything. The fewer people who know the better," she says.

Mac and Colt agree and move to head out. My eyes lock with Sage. "I'm not going anywhere," I say to her.

I've been through this with her, and she knows that I know what to do. She doesn't know, however, the pull I feel toward this girl.

Sage looks at me for a moment then nods her head. She looks back at the girl, and neither of us attempts to move. I let Sage take the lead since I know this girl is likely to trust her over me. For some reason, that kills me. I push the thought aside to review later.

"What's your name?" Sage asks her gently.

The girl looks at her, trying to decide if she can trust her. She doesn't move and doesn't speak for a few long moments. When she does, I can tell she's terrified.

"Listen, I'm sorry I trespassed. I just needed a place to rest my eyes. I didn't think anyone would find me before I moved on. I'll be out of your hair. I promise not to bother you again." She tries to stand, but I can see so much pain on her face.

"Stop. Sit. We aren't going to hurt you, and we aren't mad, at least not at you. The bastard who did this to you is another story," I say gently.

Her eyes snap to me, and my heart breaks. Behind her black bruises are the most stunning green eyes I've ever seen. She looks back to Sage and then back to me.

"This is our ranch," Sage continues. "We live in the house right there. Our parents live in the house just that way." She points toward our parents' house. "Are you from around here?"

The girl shakes her head.

"Okay, I know you don't know me, and I know you don't trust us, but I promise we won't hurt you. I have a shotgun shell reserved for the guy who did this to you should he try to set foot on our property," Sage says, and I can't help but smirk. She's come a long way, and I know she's the perfect one to help this girl.

"We've just finished breakfast. Please come in and eat, maybe get a shower, some fresh clothes, some painkillers, and rest?" Sage says. "At the very least, heal for a day or two. Then I'll take you anywhere you want to go, I promise."

The thought of this girl leaving doesn't sit very easy with me, but one thing at a time. We need to get her inside, then Sage can share her story and try to convince her to stay. She has to stay.

The girl is still looking between the two of us.

"Sage makes the best food in the whole state, and she always makes too much. We have coffee too, or Jack Daniel's, if you need a shot stronger than caffeine," I say to her.

Her lips tilt up just slightly, and I feel like puffing my chest out. I did that.

"Okay, if you're sure it's not any trouble, I don't want to put you out," she says.

I feel relieved at least that she'll stay even for a few hours. It gives us time to convince her to stick around.

"I promise," Sage says. "Plus, it will be great to have another girl around." She winks at her.

"My name is Riley," the girl says.

Riley. The sweetest name I've ever heard. It fits her.

Sage stands to help Riley up. As I watch, I see she's in more pain than she lets on.

"Sage, she won't make it down the ladder," I say.

"I'll be fine. Isn't going down easier than climbing up?" Riley asks. Strong and independent.

I stand and walk over to offer her a hand up. She shakes her head.

"Listen, it's okay to accept help. This barn is big, and you can't even stand without pain. Let us help you, please," I plead.

I see the moment she relents on her face. She takes my hand and almost as soon as she's standing, she starts to collapse. Her face gets even paler if that's even possible.

I swoop in and pick her up bridal style and walk toward the other end of the barn toward the ladder. This barn is the smaller one on the ranch, but it's still over 125-feet long. It's smaller than the length of a football field, but not by much. We keep the ladder to the front of the barn.

One way in and out at the top but you can still jump the railing in an emergency. We don't want to make it easy to get to the hayloft and play around. I'm regretting that decision now.

I stand by the ladder, trying to figure the best way to get her down, swearing about not putting a lift in by now. What is it with this barn?

"I promise I can climb down myself," Riley says.

I gently set her down, and she sits on the floor by the ladder. I glance at Sage and take a deep breath.

"Let me go first, so I can help you, okay?" I say.

She nods, and I head down the ladder.

Sage helps her down, and I can see the pain all over her face. A vice clenches around my heart. Soon as I can reach her, I gently grab her off the ladder and carry her toward the house, with Sage right behind me. The day's work forgotten; Riley is our priority today.

"Text Mac and let him know we're out of the barn so the guys can get back in there," I tell Sage.

"On it," she says.

"Sorry for causing so many problems," Riley whispers.

I look at her and smile. "No problems. I just figured you wouldn't want a bunch of rowdy ranch hands asking a load of questions just yet."

She doesn't say anything, but Sage grabs the kitchen door, and we head into the house. I start to head upstairs when I hear Sage say, "Where are you going?"

"I'm taking her upstairs to get her cleaned up," I say.

"Blaze set her down at the table. Let's get some food in her so she can take some pain meds."

I set her down at the table in what is normally my seat.

"When was the last time you ate?" I ask her.

"I got a scrap of a burger last night behind a bar, I think," she says.

I let out a growl. She shouldn't be scrounging for scraps. That won't be happening again; I'll make sure of it.

"Blaze, you're going to scare the poor girl. This isn't a time to go all caveman on her," Sage scolds.

Sage fixes her a plate and hands her a bottle of water then heads back to bring me a cup of coffee and sits down. "Dig in," Sage says to Riley, and sips at her coffee.

"Thank you," Riley says and then starts eating.

"Is there someone we can call for you?" Sage asks.

"No. Everyone I know is back home, and I can't go back." I frown. She has nowhere to go. I glance at Sage, and I can tell she's thinking the same thing I am. She'll stay here. We'll protect her.

"Please tell us what happened. How did you get here?"

Riley is hesitant. "Well, I saw an opening and ran. It took me a while to get to the interstate, and I tried to hitchhike. I got lucky; a semi pulled over. The super-nice lady had a delivery near here last night. I told her I was going to a friend's house and got out here at her stop. I ended up behind a bar, was able to get a bite to eat, and then..." she trails off.

Sage places a gentle hand on her arm. "It's okay."

Riley takes a deep breath. "Then I heard some guys stumble into the parking lot fighting. I freaked out. I jumped in the back of a pickup truck and hid. There were some blankets, so I covered myself. I must have passed out because the next thing I knew, the truck started. I was in so much pain on the bumpy road, I don't know how I stayed quiet. When the truck stopped, I waited until the coast was clear and climbed out, and ran into the barn. I was planning to rest and wait until dark and run again."

Sage never takes her eyes off Riley. "Sounds like you ended up in the back of my brother Jason's truck. He owns the bar," Sage says. "I'm glad you did. Am I right to assume you have nowhere to go? You're just running?"

Riley nods.

"Okay, this is fate. You'll stay with us," I say.

"Oh no, I can't do that. What if Jed shows up? I can't be here. He can't find me. I have to get as far away as I can."

Jed. I hate that name. He won't get near her again; I'll make sure of it.

"Where are you from?" Sage asks.

"South of Houston."

"That's around six hours away." Sage meets my gaze and adds, "Listen, you don't have to make any choices now. Promise me you'll stay for a few days and at least rest. Get to know us a bit before you run. I'll take you anywhere you want to go, even if it's Alaska. Okay? I want to see Alaska, so please say Alaska!"

Riley lets out a small laugh. "Okay, two days."

No way in hell is she going to Alaska. No way is she leaving. I'll do everything I can to make her want to stay.

Wait, what?!

I don't know this girl, but I do know I'll protect her. No girl deserves to have a guy lay a hand on her.

"Riley, my momma raised me right, and I know this isn't good manners to ask, but I have to. How old are you?"

"I understand. You have to make sure you don't have to legally turn me over, right?" Riley asks, and I nod.

"I'm twenty-three. My ID is in my purse." She nods toward the purse Sage brought in with us.

"Okay, good. I promise no one will hurt you here. We have a gate with a keypad lock, and we don't take kindly to strangers showing up. If this Jed guy gets any bright ideas, he won't make it very far, I promise," I say to her.

"You ready to take a shower and get cleaned up?" Sage asks, and Riley nods. "Blaze, will you take her to my room, please? I'm going to call Jason and Megan and let them know what's going on."

I nod and stand to pick Riley up and head upstairs.

Chapter 4

Riley

I take in Sage's house. It's huge but comfy at the same time. The side door we came in opens into the kitchen and a family dining room to the right. As Blaze carries me into the main part of the house, I see a huge formal dining room on the left.

We head up the grand staircase to a long hallway.

"The west side of the house is all guest suites," Blaze says and tilts his head to the left.

We head to the right. He tells me the first door on the right is Mac's room. To the right of his, in front of the stairs, is Megan's room. The first door on the left is Jason's room. To the left of Mac's on the right side of the hall is his room, and across from it next to Jason's is Colt's room. Sage's room is at the end of the hall.

Blaze says he and Mac share a Jack and Jill bath as do Jason and Colt, and Megan has her own because she refuses to share with the guys. I don't blame the girl.

"Why does Sage get the master?" I ask.

Blaze smiles. "It's her house, but more than that is her story to tell."

I feel oddly comfortable with Blaze. The fact that my heart is racing must be due to the last forty-eight hours, and the excruciating pain.

We walk into Sage's room, and my jaw drops. It's HUGE. Bigger than the trailer Jed and I shared. The room is light and airy and has a sitting area, a TV, bookshelves, and a huge bathroom.

Blaze sets me down on the couch—yes, a couch in her bedroom—and sits next to me.

I was terrified when I woke up and saw four people standing over me, three of them being guys. Now, sitting here with Blaze, I know I should be worried, but I feel relaxed. My gut says he's a good person, but I thought that about Jed too.

My gut is obviously a traitor and shouldn't be trusted under any circumstances.

I hear someone coming down the hall and tense up. Blaze notices and puts his hand on my arm. I flinch away.

"It's okay, it's just Sage," he says as she walks into the room.

"Okay, let's get her to the bathroom," Sage says.

Blaze picks me up again and carries me to the bathroom. I want to tell him I'm a big girl and can walk, but I'm pretty sure I wouldn't make it.

Blaze sits me down on the counter in the bathroom. Like Sage's bedroom, it's bright and looks like it's recently been redone. There's a large soaking tub and a walk-in shower with several showerheads, including a rain one from the ceiling.

The floor is covered in stone. There's a huge counter with two sinks and a door that leads to a massive closet.

I'd be okay to live in this bathroom for the rest of my life; it's huge.

Sage walks over to Blaze and shoves him out of the room.

"What are you doing? I'm not going anywhere," Blaze growls at Sage.

Yes, growls.

"Blaze, you can sit in my room, but I need to assess her injuries. That means removing clothes, and she's a girl, and you're a boy. Do we need the birds and the bees talk?"

Blaze walks backward toward the door and mumbles something to Sage, then he looks back up to me.

"I'll be right outside this door if you need anything, okay?" Blaze says to me.

The look in his eyes causes my mind to go blank, so I just nod.

NO! *Bad, Riley*. You just left one asshole guy, you're NOT looking for anything close to a relationship. No room for even a crush, even if Blaze is a completely drool-worthy cowboy, muscles, and all.

Sage closes and locks the door. "I need to ask you some questions and look at your injuries to make sure you're okay, but I know this will be uncomfortable. I think we should take pictures of the injuries, so if you choose to press charges later, we have the proof."

I start to panic. "I can't press charges. He'll find me!"

"Riley, it's okay. I know exactly how you feel."

"No, you don't," I mumble. There's no way she knows how terrified I was with every step I took. How terrified I still am that he'll find me. One slipup, and it's over. I go back, and I know he'll kill me this time if the last beating is anything to go by.

"Here, turn around and face the mirror." She turns me to face the mirror while sitting on the counter.

"May I take your hair out and brush it? I promise to be gentle," she asks.

I nod.

"Let me tell you a little about me and my story," she says while she takes my hair out.

"Blaze is my brother, but he was my best friend first. We aren't related by blood. His parents adopted me, Colt, and Mac. I was adopted about thirteen years ago."

True to her word, she's gentle as she brushes my hair and tries to work out all the knots.

"I was born in this house with my bio parents, aka my sperm and egg donor. I was supposed to be a boy, carry the family name, take over the ranch. I wasn't, so they tried again for a boy. The harder it was for them to get pregnant, the more my sperm donor drank and the more abusive he got. Once they finally got their boy, he was the king of the castle and could do no wrong. The abuse got worse. Blaze and his family lived next door. We had been friends since we were in diapers." She meets my eyes in the mirror.

"Blaze found out about the abuse in the same way we found you today. I was hiding and trying to stay out of my sperm donor's way while he was drunk. Blaze panicked, I know that now. But I was terrified of entering the foster care system. Of losing Blaze. He was my rock; still is. I made him swear not to tell his parents, not to tell anyone. It took some convincing, but he promised. After that, I learned how to stay out of the old man's way. I played the system, said what I knew he wanted to hear."

She took a deep breath. "The first time Blaze found me, I was six. A year later, I was in the wrong place at the wrong time and got a beating worse than before, and hid in the barn again. This time, Blaze and Colt found me. Now, it's not my story to tell, but Colt had a similar home life. The three of us bonded, and Colt became just as protective as Blaze. Over the next two years, they were my guardian angels. Saved me from a few beatings, but I had bruises daily and faced several more serious beatings. Some broken bones, ribs, busted lips, a black eye or two. Blaze and Colt covered for me for each time."

"Then one day, I was heading home with Blaze, and I could hear the old man screaming from the tree line over by the barn. I panicked. I begged Blaze not to send me home. He took me back to his house and hid me in the den and snuck me out before his parents woke up. This happened for several months before his mom found out. His mom then went to my sperm donor, and I don't know what the conversation was, but she wanted him to sign over guardianship. He refused. When I came home from school I got the worst beating ever. I almost died that day. Blaze and Colt stopped him. Blaze took a few hits from him as did Colt, but they saved my life. They got me back to Blaze's parents and we took pictures, called the cops. It took me a bit before I'd open up about everything that happened. Blaze's parents took me in and once my sperm donor went to jail, they were able to adopt me a year later."

I listen to everything she says. Then she's quiet, leaving me to my thoughts while she continues to brush my hair. It's strangely calming.

"Why move back into this house with all the bad memories?" I ask her.

"My sperm donor was a horrible person, but my grandparents were amazing. They worked hard for this land. My bio brother has taken after his old man and is a piece of shit, he wants nothing to do with it. When they ran it to the ground, I wanted it. It should have been mine by birthright, being the oldest, but they would never give it to me. We knew it would go up for sale. Mom and Dad and my siblings, we all busted our butts to save up for it."

"They let the property and the house get into such a state that we bought it for cheaper than we thought we would. We used the extra money to remodel the house from top to bottom. It looks nothing like it did then, even the layout has moved around. I begged the guys and Megan to move in with me. If they had told me no, then I wouldn't have moved in. I couldn't live here alone."

I nod. I understand that. I take a deep breath. She knows where I'm coming from, to an extent. My parents died when I was a teen, but I always knew they loved me. I just have a shitty taste in guys. I can't imagine a childhood growing up and knowing the two people who should love you no matter almost killed you.

"I know you may not want to press charges, and I get it, but we won't let him touch you again. All five of us are great shots, and we love moving targets." She winks at me via the mirror. "But please let me take pictures, so we have them when you change your mind. Because you will change your mind."

I take a deep breath. I need the proof, I know that. If she could do this at eleven or twelve, then I can do it now at twenty-three. I nod. Sage pulls out her phone, sends off a quick text, then opens the camera. She pulls my hair back gently into a ponytail.

"Turn and face me. We'll start with your face," she says.

I do as she says, and she takes a photo from the front and both sides of my face. Then she asks me to stand, but I have to lean on the counter behind me. She takes a full body picture.

"Let's remove your shirt and pants. We'll wash them, and I'll give you some of my clothes to wear. Is that okay?"

I nod. I'm thankful she gives me a choice. She's gentle, and I feel safe. For the first time in four years, I feel safe. I undress and leave my bra and underwear on.

Sage takes pictures of the bruises on my legs and arms and the nasty ones on my ribs before having me turn around to take pictures of the ones on my back.

"Blaze called our family doctor. Please let us take you to see him and make sure nothing internal is wrong."

"No, I'm fine," I say.

"You're in so much pain. Plus, we need this documented more than just photos. Don't worry about the cost; we'll cover it. Please do this for us, for our peace of mind."

"I can't pay you back right now. I have forty dollars to my name, and no one will hire me like this. But I'll pay you back." I sigh.

"Well, when you're feeling a bit better, we can talk about you working here at the ranch with us and working it off. The job comes with room and board, and a paycheck."

"You don't even know if I know anything about ranch work!" I say.

"Do you? Can you cook? Can you clean?" Sage asks as she walks into her closet and rummages around.

"Well, my parents owned a ranch before they died. I picked some of it up. I can cook, but I've been told I'm not very good. Cleaning I can do."

"See, we can find a spot for you. I need to get a cook and someone to help clean this place, but if that's not you, that's okay. We need help in the barn and with the horses just as bad," Sage says, coming out with some clothes.

"I don't have a new bra, but these panties still have the tags, and we can adjust this dress so it fits you. I've a sweater we can put over it to hide the bruises on your arms when we head into town. Some sunglasses will complete the look. No one will know! Then in town, we can grab you some clothes and other essentials." Sage pulls out a towel and washcloth.

"Here you go, take a shower or a bath. Use anything you need in the shower and on the counter. There's a new toothbrush in the medicine cabinet. Take as long as you want. Blaze and I will wait in my room, okay?"

I nod. "Sage, I can't thank you enough for this."

"I'm paying it forward from the ones who helped me. Don't be afraid to ask for help. I'm here for anything."

Sage steps out and allows me to take a bath.

Chapter 5

Blaze

I see Sage finally step out of the bathroom and jump up.

"How is she? Did you get pictures? Did she agree to see the doctor? Is she going to press charges? Is she going to stay? What happened?" I fire off at Sage.

"Whoa! Easy, tiger!" Sage throws her hands up and then collapses on the couch. I sit back down next to her, and she lies down with her legs over my lap. This is normal for us to sit like this and watch TV at night, but I'm much too worked up to be patient.

"She's okay, all things considered. I did get pictures. As for pressing charges, I think she will, but not right now. She's still terrified. I told her my story, and it seemed to calm her down. She's agreed to go to the doctor. She refused at first, due to not being able to pay for it but I said we would cover it and she could work it off on the ranch once she feels better. She agreed. I think she wants to help with the horses."

I smiled at that. She's going to stay. I don't know why I'm so relieved. I tell myself it's because I can keep an eye on her, and she'll be safe. My heart wants to tell a different story; it says I need more time, I need to see a full-on smile from her.

Behind the bruises, I can tell she's drop-dead gorgeous. I have to tell myself she won't want anything to do with guys for a long time. But I'm stubborn. I'll prove myself, no matter how long it takes.

Sage and I make plans for the next few days. We agree we need to tell Mom and Dad what's going on and to put Riley in the guest room next to Megan. They can share a bathroom. We also agree on both of us taking her to the doctor and shopping for clothes and other things she needs.

I can tell Sage won't admit it, but she wants me there in case this guy Riley is afraid of shows up.

We aren't sure exactly what happened or if there's any way for him to track her here, but it's best to be overly cautious than to blow it off, and then something happens. We promised to take care of her, and we'll do just that.

We then switch gears and talk about ranch work. We agree to tell the guys to be on extra alert. No strangers are to be on the property, and any visitors for the next week or so are canceled. Make sure they carry a shotgun with them.

Most do anyway; you never know what you'll find in the fields. Coyotes and wolves are common, and cattle rustlers like to push their luck from time to time as well.

We also agree to have some guys do a perimeter fence run to make sure everything is set and to turn on the perimeter electric fence for extra safety. We'll also lock doors and triple-check them all and make sure we set the alarm at night.

I don't say anything, but I'm also going to be sleeping in the lounge area right off the stairs on the second story with my gun. I know how crazy Sage's sperm donor got when he saw he was losing her. I can only imagine how this boyfriend could get. I won't take any chances.

Ex-boyfriend, I correct myself.

Then a thought pops in my head.

"Do you think we should leave her to sleep alone? The guest room next to Megan's is too close to the stairs. He could get in and out without passing any of us," I say.

"Good point," Sage says and looks up at the ceiling. "She'll stay in here with me then. You all should sleep with your doors open as well. It won't be easy getting past the four of you."

I nod in agreement. Then we hear the bathroom door open. We stand and look toward Riley.

My knees go weak, and I find it hard to breathe as I look at her. Cleaned up with her hair brushed down, it has a slight curl to it. She's in a black maxi dress I've seen on Sage many times. On Riley, it's stunning.

"Let me grab that sweater and a pair of sandals for you to wear, and we'll head to town," Sage says.

Riley looks nervous about leaving the house. I walk over to her slowly. No sudden movement, I remember that from my time with Sage. No matter how much she trusted me, sudden movements were still too much for her.

"I'm going with you to town. I won't leave your side, I promise," I say.

She nods and gives a slightly forced smile. Sage comes out and hands Riley a pink sweater, sandals, and oversized sunglasses. After Riley puts them all on you can't see a single bruise. Now I get the outfit choice and smile at her.

"Perfect," I tell her "No one will think anything of it, other than the sweater is a bit much in the Texas heat."

Sage laughs. "Come on, Mom brings a sweater everywhere. Claims everyone has their air too cold inside!" She pulls a handgun from her closet and checks it. We all have carry permits, and I know we'll be using them more often now.

"Yes, she does," I agree.

Riley looks scared. "We all have a carry permit and will have a gun on us at all times until *Jed...*" I spit out his name, "is behind bars."

I watch Riley relax a bit.

"Ready?" I ask Riley and hold my arm out for her to hold.

She nods. Her steps are slow, and she's breathing a bit harder than she should be, but she handles it well until we get to the stairs. Without a second thought, I scoop her up and carry her down. I don't set her down until we get to the passenger seat of my truck.

I turn around and see a strange look on Sage's face. She looks at me and then smiles.

I don't like this smile. This is the one she gets when she has something up her sleeve. The one that means trouble. The smile is even worse when it's directed at me.

Shit.

I walk around to the driver's side, expecting Sage to do the same and sit in the middle of the bench seat. Instead, when I get in, I hear Sage talking to Riley.

"Hey, scoot over a bit to the middle and let a girl in," Sage says to Riley, a wicked smile on her face.

"Sage, why don't you sit in the middle?" I ask her.

"This way, I can see both of you when I'm talking," she says.

Oh, she's up to something, and I don't think I'm going to like it.

During the drive into town, Sage and Riley talk about what she knows ranch wise. We learn her parents owned a ranch in south Texas, but they and her brother died in a car crash when she was sixteen. She ended up in her aunt's home where she was ignored until she turned eighteen and could move out on her own.

She didn't get the chance to move out. Her aunt kicked her out on her eighteenth birthday.

She then got a job waiting tables and slept on a friend's couch, trying to save money. That's how she met Jed. Then she clams up; she doesn't want to talk about anything relating to him. I can't say I blame her.

Sage tells her a bit about how she and the guys all came into the family. She doesn't go into much detail, but she tells her about her traveling after graduation and then how the ranch came up for sale and how we bought it and turned it around.

We arrive at the doctor's office, and I park the truck and run over to open the door to help Riley out. She insists on walking into the office, but I can tell it takes all her strength. She collapses into the first chair she comes upon.

Sage goes to the receptionist and checks us in, as I sit next to Riley.

Sage sits next to me but leans forward to look at Riley. "You okay, girl?" she asks.

"I don't know if I can do this," Riley barely whispers.

"Don't worry. I won't leave your side, not for one minute," Sage replies.

"I'll be right here waiting for you, I promise," I say, knowing very well Sage won't let me back there with them, no matter what I say. I'll save the fight for later.

A nurse steps into the waiting room. "Sage?" she asks.

Riley and Sage stand. Sage puts her arm around Riley's waist to help her, and they disappear behind the door leading to the back.

Now it's time to wait. I've never been a very patient person.

I pull out my phone and browse my emails, scroll Facebook, read the news, and text Mom and Dad, who are asking questions about Riley and how it's going.

I text Colt and Mac to check up on the ranch and tell them to make sure to run the perimeter fence ASAP so we can flip on the electricity. They text me back that they're already on it with orders from Sage.

I don't know when she found time to text them, but I'm grateful.

Nearly forty-five minutes have passed. I text Sage to see how it's going.

Me: Any updates?

Sage: They did some x-rays. She has three broken ribs, but they didn't puncture anything.

Me: Shit.

Sage: The nurses took some blood from her for testing, and they took pictures. They did some other tests and there doesn't seem to be anything internal to worry about.

Me: Good. How's she holding up?

Sage: She's a champ. We're waiting for the Dr. to come back but B, she has had several other breaks that didn't heal right. From what I can tell, this has been going on for about four years.

That makes me fume.

Four years?

Did she try to get out before? Was she able to? Did no one else notice in her hometown? How could no one care?

Sage: Dr. is back. Chat later.

With so much running through my mind, I get up and pace the waiting room, which earns me a look from Mrs. Miller the receptionist. I'm sure that will feed the beauty shop gossip for a few days.

Megan!

I pull my phone back out and shoot a text off to Megan.

Me: Hey, any gossip about Riley in the shop?

Megan: No, not yet. Why?

Me: I just want to stay on top of it. Will you let me know what they say?

Megan: Of course, big brother. How's she doing?

Me: She's back with the Dr. right now. Few broken ribs, lots of bruises, but she'll be okay.

Megan: Good. Oh, the next client is here. See you at dinner!

Me: Have fun.

I start to put my phone away as it goes off again.

Sage: Dr. is wrapping up. Be out soon.

I sit back down and wait for them.

The rest of the day goes by uneventfully. It takes a lot of talking to get Riley to pick out clothes. She'll only let us get her a week's worth. But I know Sage; she has her sizes now and will buy her more. We stop at the big box store, even though, I hate shopping and while they stock up on bras, panties, and socks, I go to fill Riley's prescriptions and get some food.

By the time the girls are done shopping, Riley has clothes, toiletries, and even makeup.

We grab lunch, but Riley doesn't want to go inside, so we eat in the truck on the way home. While I hate shopping, I have a great time spending it with my girls.

Whoa. My girls?

Chapter 6

Riley

Once we get back, the painkillers the doctor has given me are working. I've got to take it easy for the next week and stay bandaged up, if the pain starts, I've got to lie down. Shopping for clothes has been enough to wipe me out for the day.

I make it up the stairs on my own for the first time since being here, and Sage shows me to the guest room next to Megan's to put my stuff away.

"While you can keep your stuff here, Blaze, and I think you should stay in my room with me."

"Why?" I ask, looking around the room. It's bigger than any room I've had in my whole life and painted in a warm blueish-gray color with a tan plush carpet. There are two floor-to-ceiling windows with light cream, almost white, curtains. They're huge and let in so much light.

On the wall to the right is a queen-size bed with matching white and blue sheets with more pillows than I would know what to do with. Above the headboard are a bunch of mirrors of all shapes and sizes put together; none of them are bigger than the size of a piece of paper. There's a nightstand on either side with matching lamps.

On the wall opposite the bed is a dresser with a TV mounted to the wall above it, and in the corner, a light-blue plush chair, and a reading lamp. There's a bench at the foot of the bed, a walk-in closet to my right, and the door to the bathroom to my left.

I'm in complete awe.

"Well, Blaze wants to make sure you're well protected if the guy happens to get in the house," Sage says.

Instant terror. Would Jed show up? How would he find me? It must have shown on my face because Sage places a hand on my arm and gives me a small smile.

"Don't worry, the guys and I are all sleeping with our guns, and they're keeping their doors open so they can hear everything. We've amped up security; we have an alarm, and if we find out he's in town, we'll set up a night watch rotation with the ranch hands. We've turned the electric fence on, and the only other way in is via the gate, and that's video monitored. We want you to feel safe here, so we might be overdoing it."

Sage removes her arms, walks to the bed, and sets the bags down. "So, are you okay sleeping in my room with me? I can take the couch, and you can have the bed. You need the rest."

"I'm okay in the room but not if you're sleeping on the couch. Your bed is huge; we can share it," I say. "I'd feel better not being alone too."

"Then it's settled. You can hang your stuff in the closet and keep your stuff here. This room is yours if you need space or want to be alone, but you'll spend the night in my room until we get everything sorted out, okay?"

I smile and nod. "How would you know if Jed is in town?" I ask.

"We're a small town, and they may gossip, but we protect our own. The grapevine gets set on fire if a stranger walks into town. Plus, my sister Megan owns and works at the beauty shop. That's gossip central, and we put her on spy duty," Sage says with a smile. "I'm going to start on dinner. Rest here and lie down. The TV remotes are in the nightstand. I'll bring you a plate for dinner."

"I'd like to come down for dinner, if possible, I haven't been part of a family dinner in years," I say. "If I won't be intruding, that is."

"You'll never be intruding. You live here now and are welcome at every meal. We'd be happy to have you, and you can meet everyone officially." Sage smiles at me.

She leaves and shuts the door. I'm alone for the first time since my bath earlier. I put the bags in my closet with the intent of unpacking them later. I lie on the bed. It's so comfortable.

I think about the turn of events in my life. My parents had always said the best things in life are the unexpected turns. I never believed them because until now, that was them dying, my aunt, and Jed.

I don't dare hope this will last. Eventually, Jed will find me, or they'll send me packing as my aunt did.

I close my eyes, and Blaze crosses my mind. Blaze.

The super-sexy cowboy who is sweet, caring, treats his sister like gold and seems to know how not to push me. According to Sage, he was there for her, so I guess he's reliving those memories.

Oh, God.

Is that all I'm around here for? A reminder of bad memories?

Sage and Blaze have been amazing. If all I'm doing is digging up old memories, I'll leave, no questions asked. I can't do that to them. They don't deserve it.

At some point, I guess I drifted off to sleep. The next thing I know, I hear someone saying my name.

I open my eyes to see Blaze.

"Hey," he says softly. He's sitting on the edge of my bed, rubbing my shoulder, waking me up. "Sage sent me to get you. Dinner is ready."

I smile and sit up slowly.

"How are you feeling?" he asks.

"Sore, but I guess I needed that nap more than I knew. I feel a lot better."

He smiles at me, and it lights up his face. My heart skips a beat.

"Come on, we have some people excited to meet you. Mom and Dad have come over too. We eat with them a few times a week. Mom cooks every Sunday at her house, and they come over here at least once a week, if not more. Many of the ranch hands will be in and out of the kitchen for food, but they won't bother us."

He helps me down the stairs as needed and is very patient but lets me do it.

Once we get to the bottom of the stairs, he leaves his hand on the small of my back and leads me to the table. I try not to make too much out of it other than the sparks keep coming from wherever his hand touches. They shoot straight to my core.

What the hell?

Bad, Riley. No.

He pulls out a chair for me to sit and takes the one next to me. Sage sits at the head of the table next to him. It's weird to see her as the head of the house with so many guys. I know her story, but I feel like there's more there.

A girl sits next to me. "Hi, I'm Megan. This guy's sister," she says and playfully punches Blaze's arm. "I own the beauty shop in town."

A guy with blond hair and the most stunning blue eyes I've ever seen sits on the other side of Megan.

"This is Hunter. He's my best friend and is always over," Megan says.

"Nice to meet you, Riley. You'll love it here; they'll treat you like family," Hunter says.

An older gentleman sits at the other end of the table across from Sage and to his left is an older woman.

Blaze leans over. "That's my Mom and Dad," he says.

The woman gets up and comes over to gently hug me. "My name is Helen. You can call me Helen. Everyone here calls me Mom, so you can call me that too if you wish. We're so happy to have you here," she says.

I'm shocked. Are they happy I'm here? I think she's just being nice, but I guess time will tell.

"I'm Tim or Dad," Blaze's Dad says.

Across the table from me are three guys. Blaze introduces the one next to his mom as Jason. The oldest of them all. Apparently, he owns the bar and it was his truck I climbed into. Next to Jason is Mac. The youngest and from a local reservation. He kind of looks like that guy the girls were swooning over in *Twilight* that turned into a wolf. And between Mac and Sage is Colt.

They all talk about the ranch and their day. They bring me into the conversation in such a natural way I barely notice, but they never push me. Asking me about my ranch experience and favorite foods, school, and work experience.

I watch everyone, taking it all in, and I notice two things. Hunter is sitting closer than need be to Megan, and his eyes sparkle when she talks. He's very attentive to her and finds small ways to touch her.

I'm willing to bet there's something there, even if they won't admit it just yet.

The second thing I notice is Colt. He's always watching Sage. He's friendly and talks to everyone, and he has been nothing but nice to me. But it's like there's a wall up between them. They seem drawn to each other and are always looking at each other when the other isn't paying attention.

After we finish eating, we're all just talking, and Helen asks about my doctor's appointment. Sage gives her the basics. But Helen and Tim seem a bit upset that I won't press charges.

"I just can't take the chance of him finding out where I am. He will make bail. No one in that town will hold him or believe me. I've tried, and it just resulted in me being dumped back at his house and things getting worse. I can't do it again."

I feel Blaze's hand rubbing my back gently.

"We won't let that happen again. You aren't someone's property, and no one can force you to go anywhere. You're an adult. We'll protect you. You don't even have to leave here if you don't want to. You have a room here and as soon as you have the doctor's okay, you have a job. You can go to school online like we did. We won't let him lay a hand on you again."

Everyone at the table agrees, and my eyes tear up. I've never known this kind of support, and I'm just a stranger. They just met me today!

"Excuse me," I say and leave the table and head up to my room.

I walk to the bathroom and find a washcloth to wipe down my face. I look in the mirror and cringe. I don't want to see myself until the bruises heal. It's too much.

I lie on the bed and hear a faint tap on my door.

"It's open," I say, expecting to see Sage or Blaze.

I'm shocked to see Mac. He smiles shyly.

"Hi, I offered to bring up your pain meds. Blaze said it was time for another dose." He walks to the bed and hands me the pill and a glass of water. "Mind if I sit? I'd like to tell you how I came into the family."

Intrigued, I nod and scoot over a bit. He sits on the side of the bed and looks at me.

"Did Sage tell you her story?" he asks me.

"Yes, though not in detail. I think she skipped over quite a bit," I say.

"Yes, she did with me too. I think Blaze and Colt only know the gory details," he says. "My story is much the same," he starts. "I grew up on the reservation, and my dad was a nasty drunk. He'd go after my sisters, and I would step in to take the heat off them, even though I was the youngest. My mom died of cancer, and my dad started drinking. I think he just couldn't deal after she died." He looks down at his hands in his lap.

I stay quiet and let him continue.

"Well, one day, I ran into Sage. Literally. She wasn't paying attention and plowed into me. She put her hand on my shoulder to steady herself, and I winced. It had been dislocated just the day before, and my sister helped me put it back in place. I had a busted lip too. I think Sage knew instantly what was going on. She had been adopted by Mom and Dad at this point. I was the new guy at school. My dad had sent me to the high school in town because the reservation teachers were getting suspicious of him and wouldn't get off his back."

He takes a deep breath. "From that moment on, Sage was a leech. I couldn't get rid of her even if I wanted to. Although, being as pretty as she is, and the only person who wanted to spend time with me, I didn't want her to leave me alone. Not that anything has ever happened between us. It's never been like that," he says like he can read my mind.

"She introduced me to Blaze and Colt, and they accepted me, no questions asked. The next day and every day after that, Sage waited for me before school and would talk about everything and nothing all at once. I knew she was taking stock of any new injures. She never pushed me and I know she told Blaze and Colt everything, even if they didn't act like they knew. She also had told Mom and Dad." I watch him, lost in thought before he continues.

"A few weeks later, I mentioned my dad was out of town on some tribe work, and my sister was staying at a friend's house. Sage insisted I come over for dinner. She got Blaze and Colt on the bandwagon and well, you know Sage. I couldn't say no. I spent most of the weekend here and fell in love with the family. I met

Megan and Jason, and we had a blast riding and swimming at the swimming hole. I forgot about the bruises and scars and went swimming. When I took my shirt off, everyone clammed up. I had several bruises on my ribs and a nasty one on my back. How I forgot, I don't know, but I just felt... normal for the first time in my life. That day changed my life. Sage hugged me and said everything would be okay and then grabbed my hand to pull me into the water with her. They didn't treat me differently. Nothing changed."

"That night, Sage came to the room I was staying in and sat on my bed much like this and told me her story. For the first time, I didn't feel alone. She showed me some pictures of her the last time her old man beat her up and told me she would be there for me, no matter what. When my old man found out where I was all weekend, I got a beating I couldn't hide. I missed school the next day. My old man spent most of the day passed out drunk, and I did schoolwork to make up for not being there. I should have known Sage would know what happened. From what the guys tell me, after the first period when they realized I wasn't there, Sage pulled Colt and

Blaze out of class and told them. She didn't waste any time getting to me.

"Unlucky for them, they got there just as my dad was waking up and taking his first drink. To save you from the gory details, let's say that Sage is a badass. She took a bullet for me and put one in my dad just as the elders showed up at the same time as the cops. It's a feeling of freedom not to be looking over your shoulder all the time."

"Sage took a bullet for you?" I ask, my eyes wide.

He smiles at me. "Yeah, she saved my life. You should ask her to see the scar. She laughs now, we all do, but we didn't back then. The elders did their best to find a place for my sister and me. My sister was a week away from her eighteenth birthday, and she bolted to escape the system. She's married now and lives in Virginia. Mom and Dad took me in, no questions asked."

"They seem like nice people," I say while I try to process everything I've been told.

"They are. I don't talk about this often, as you can imagine, but I want you to know, this family, the people at the table tonight? They understand. They've put their lives on the line before and will do it again gladly. You might not know it yet, but you're part of us now. I see it in Sage's eyes and even Blaze's." He stands and pats my shoulder. "Welcome home." He smiles at me, then turns and walks out.

I lie on the bed thinking of Mac's story for a while until another knock lands on my door and Blaze peeks his head in.

"Hey, Sage and I are heading to her room to watch TV. Want to join us?"

"Sure, let me change into my PJs. The meds will probably knock me out soon."

"Okay, just meet us in her room when you're ready."

I get up and change into the black loose yoga-like pants Sage swears by and a t-shirt. I pull my hair into a loose braid over my shoulder and head down to Sage's room.

Her door is open, so I peek my head in. Blaze smiles at me.

"Hey, come get comfy. We were just debating what to watch," Blaze says.

"Why don't you take the bed?" Sage says.

I nod in agreement and really take in her room this time. It's huge, almost three times the size of my room. *I think my room is huge...*

The walls are painted the faintest yellow, and the whole room has teal accents. There are huge, exposed wood beams in the ceiling, and the room has the same almost floor-to-ceiling windows like mine, just more of them.

Walking in, her huge king-size bed is to the right, framed by windows, and to the left is her bathroom and the huge closet I remember. Is there a size bigger than a king? I think her bed is the next size up! At the foot of her bed is a bench just like my room. Apparently, that's a thing around here.

Across the room is a beautiful stone fireplace with a huge TV above it. The chairs are done in the same teal color as the room, and there's a cream loveseat and sofa completing the seating area. A beautiful chandelier hangs in the center of the room with a wrought-iron chain and lights made to look like flickering candles.

I'm too busy taking in the room, I don't notice Sage coming up to me.

"This is my dream room. I spent months pouring over home magazines. When I had more than one idea, I turned the others into the guest rooms. I let the guys and Megan each design their own rooms though. Give them their own space, though Blaze seems to spend more time in here than his room," Sage jokes.

"Well, you do have the good TV." Blaze laughs.

I notice Blaze is in sweatpants that hug his hips snuggly, and he has no shirt on. His abs are ripped, the kind of definition that shows he definitely doesn't shy away from hard work. My mouth goes dry, and I'm frozen in place.

"Blaze put on a shirt. You're making the girl uncomfortable," Sage says, but I swear there's amusement under her stern order.

Blaze gets up grumbling and heads to his room.

I settle down in the bed, and Sage says they're going to watch the latest episode from their favorite TV show, *Supernatural.*

I haven't heard of it; I wasn't allowed to watch TV. When Blaze comes back, and the show starts, I can see the appeal—two hot demon-chasing brothers. *Yum*; it's the last thought I have as I drift off to sleep.

Chapter 7

Blaze

Riley has been here for a week now. Yesterday, the doctor gave approval for her to be up and moving around. No lifting, but she doesn't have to follow Sage's strict bedrest policy. After the doctor's appointment, the girls go shopping for more clothes. Sage insists that Riley has a proper 'uniform' to work with the horses.

I think it's just an excuse to buy her more clothes. She has bought her jeans, shirts, a pair of boots and a cowgirl hat.

I smile, thinking of Riley settling in at the ranch. She's excited because Sage is letting her sit in on the horse training today. While she still can't do much, she can watch and learn.

Riley has been staying nights in Sage's room, which works out great. It seems neither of them likes being alone, so they're helping each other. Riley's bruises are pretty much gone, and there has been no sign of the bastard ex of hers.

Each day, Riley seems to relax just a tiny bit. She's laughing and joking more and even wanting to help with the cooking.

Sage, Colt, Jason, and I are at the table eating breakfast when Riley walks in. My heart stops, then kicks back up, running as fast as an out-of-control race car.

Riley's in jeans that look like they're painted on and a teal plaid button-down shirt with a matching teal tank under it. It must be Sage's doing; that's her favorite color. She has matched it with a brown leather belt and brown cowgirl boots with teal stitching. In her hand is a brown with matching teal band cowgirl hat.

Hot damn, this girl is fucking hot.

I'm a goner. I'm in so much trouble. I want nothing more than to take her to dinner and convince her to stay and never leave, but the last thing she needs is a guy's attention.

I'm fucked.

She grabs breakfast and sits next to me. Sage kicks me under the table and knocks me out of the lust fog I'm in.

I continue to eat, still unable to speak.

"Are you excited to watch Sage with the horses?" Jason asks.

"Yeah, I love horses, although I haven't ridden in almost ten years. I know I won't be on a horse for probably two more months, but I'm really excited." Riley smiles at Jason and for the first time ever, I want to sucker punch my brother for winning that smile instead of me.

I sip my coffee and decide to check some of the back cattle fields today, to keep myself busy.

"Well, I'm out to the back east if anyone needs me. I see y'all at dinner." I head out and Colt follows behind me, grabbing something to eat, and walking with me.

"Want some help? You look like something is on your mind," Colt says.

"Yeah, if you don't mind being ignored while I sort through it," I say.

He smiles because he gets it. He's been working through his own stuff lately.

We saddle up our horses and load them into the trailer. Since the back fields are so far away, it makes sense to drive out and save the horse's energy.

As I'm getting into the truck, I feel my phone go off.

Sage: Next time, wipe the drool off your face.

"Fucking Sage," I mumble, sending the middle finger emoji back at her.

Beside me, Colt laughs. "She's always been able to read you like an open book, though you were kind of obvious at the table this morning."

My phone goes off again. I almost ignore it, but no matter how much Sage irritates me, she's my best friend, and I've never ignored her.

Sage: Hey, I approve but go easy and ease her into the idea, okay? I don't think she has a great impression of men.

Me: I know, and I don't even know what I think right now.

Sage: Hence, why you're heading to the back-east fields. Hash it out with Colt, and I'll see you at dinner.

Me: See ya.

I put my phone away and shake my head.

"She can read you like a book, huh?" Colt says beside me as we head out.

"Always has been able to. She can read you too, ya know," I say, hoping to flip the attention to him.

"Not lately," he says almost bitterly.

"What do you mean?"

"It seems like neither of us can read the other anymore. I think she's going left, and she goes right. It's like she does it just to piss me off."

"She probably does." I chuckle back at him.

"Yeah, and you're hating how well she knows you right now," he fires back.

I grunt but don't say anything else on the drive out to the fields.

As we check cattle and run the fence lines, I can't seem to get my mind off Riley; the pretty blond who has stormed into our lives and turned them upside down. I want to know about her past, even the details with the ex. I feel like I need to know, so I know what I'm up against.

I want to show her how she should be treated, even if she walks away. She needs to know how a woman should be treated when she wants to date again.

There's a pain in my gut at the thought of Riley walking away, of there being a 'next' guy. The thought of seeing her with another guy is like a knife in the gut.

Have I gone crazy? I've known this girl for a week.

I spend the rest of the day working, talking with Colt, and trying to keep my mind off the blonde who has captured my attention, who is waiting back at the house.

• • • ● • ● • • •

We fall into a comfortable routine over the next week, and I make it my mission to let Riley get to know me and get to know whatever she's willing to share with me.

I'm lying in bed one night after watching TV with Sage and Riley, just thinking about how I can get an extra few minutes in with Riley this weekend without scaring her off when my bedroom door creaks open.

I sit up on my bed and know already it's Sage; she's the only person in this house who doesn't knock. She shuts my bedroom door and sits next to me on the bed.

"What's wrong? Is Riley okay?" I ask.

"Yes, she fell asleep. I wanted to talk to you."

We settle against my headboard next to each other. We've spent many nights like this talking or just sitting here.

"You like Riley," Sage says. It isn't a question. She knows me, sometimes better than I know myself. I don't bother trying to deny it. "What are you going to do about it?"

"I don't know. I'm sure being with a guy is the last thing on her mind. Plus, it's going to be ten times harder to earn her trust simply because I'm a guy."

"You don't know that."

"Sage, I know you were a lot younger when everything happened to you, but you didn't trust guys easily. How long was it before you had a real relationship? Colt and I were the only ones you let in. You even kept Jason at arm's length until Mac came in the picture."

"I dated in high school!" Sage said.

"Yeah? Who? You didn't have any relationships until you came back home, and we bought the ranch. Even then, you still give bullshit reasons why you would break up with the guys. I love you and support you, but you're still one who doesn't trust easily."

"Blaze, you're so clueless sometimes, but this isn't about me. Stop deflecting. We need a plan."

"I'm not clueless, and we need nothing."

"Listen, I've spent every day with Riley. I may not trust easily, but I do trust my gut.

You two are perfect for each other."

"Well, convince her of that, would ya?"

She smiles at me. "Oh, I plan to. Just take things slow and maybe flirt a little. Ease her into it and when I finally push you to date, don't fight me. Got it?"

"Sage, I can handle this on my own, thank you."

"Really? Then why haven't you?"

I grunt. I know I've lost the argument.

Sage kisses my cheek and heads back to her room.

I don't get much sleep as I ponder what Sage might have up her sleeve.

Chapter 8

Riley

The last few weeks have been some of the best I can remember in my life. My bruises are gone, and my ribs have healed, though I have the final doctor follow-up next week.

I've been learning how Sage handles the horses. I've mostly been watching her working while she tells me why she does this and that, and she quizzes me. She has been letting me help her with feedings and bringing her lighter items.

I've been helping her cook. It's been an adjustment to learn how to cook meals for twenty-plus people, so the ranch hands have food. I love that they've let me try out a few recipes I've found online.

Sage has let me use her computer to look up schools and try to figure out what I want to study. I've also been keeping an eye on the news for any sign of Jed or any news on myself.

I'm still spending nights in Sage's room, and it's been a nightly routine where Blaze, Sage, and I watch TV. They have me addicted to *Supernatural* and were more than happy to start the series from the beginning for me. We get in one episode a night, some nights even two. We've just started season three now. Apparently, they're on season fifteen, so I've got a ways to go to catch up.

The one thing that's constantly on my mind is Blaze. He's been sweet and respectful. He's always near me when he's around. Plus, come on, he isn't bad to look at.

Sage seems to always mention something about Blaze daily. Telling me about how they came up with the plan to buy the ranch, how he worked his butt off for her dream, how he met her at the Grand Canyon, how he helped her with her nightmares.

I've been telling myself I don't want a relationship, but hell, who am I lying to? What I should say is I don't *need* a relationship. I have a lot I need to do.

I need to stand on my own two feet.

I need to pay Sage back.

I need to figure out what I want to go to school for.

I need to figure out if I can stay here.

I need to figure out Jed's next move. I'm not stupid enough to think this is over. He won't give up that easy. He never has.

But that hasn't stopped me from wanting to get to know Blaze better, from wanting to spend time with him. It hasn't stopped my heart from kicking into gear when he looks at me and smiles.

"So, any idea what you want to do with your hair?" Sage brings me back to reality.

I've mentioned to Megan I could use a haircut, and she has suggested I come to the shop. I told her I wasn't ready so she's going to cut my hair when she gets home tonight. I'm excited; it's been almost a year since I've been able to get my hair done.

"I want to keep it long, but the dead ends need to be fixed. I'd like some layers and shape. Nothing too fancy, I think."

"Talk with Megan. She's good at giving ideas based on your face shape. I swear she should be working in Hollywood with the stars, but she has no desire to leave home. Owning a salon is the next best option."

She then, not too subtlety, switches topics to Blaze again. "So, do you like my brother?" My jaw drops.

"What?" I ask to make sure I heard her correctly.

"You heard me. I'm not blind. I see how you two look at each other. For the record, I like that idea. I think you would be good for him, and I wouldn't protest at having you for a sister."

"Look, I'm far from being ready for a relationship. I have no idea how to pick good guys. My high school boyfriend broke up with me when my parents died. My prom date was only with me to get laid. Then there's Jed, the mother of all mistakes."

Sage walks over to me and stands on the other side of the fence. "I get it. People like us have trust issues with men. But take this to heart and learn it from me, now and not years down the road when it's too late, and the guy for you slips away. Trust your gut. It will tell you who the good ones are. I bet if you think back to those guys, there were red flags you ignored?"

I look away because I've thought about it many times, and she's right. Jed always said I was desperate to be loved and he was desperate to love, so we made a great pair. He was right about me, at least, even though he was wrong about the rest of it.

After my parents died, all I wanted was the love I had from them. My aunt barely looked my way. The guys I dated weren't it. I thought Jed was. He gave me the moon and the stars at first, but I didn't realize that by giving me everything I wanted, he stripped my independence, isolating me so he could control me. I won't make that mistake again.

Then I think back to Sage's words. "You let your guy slip away? Is it too late to fix?" I ask.

She stares off toward the barn, and I begin to think she won't answer when she speaks softly.

"I messed up and ran because he said he loved me. At that point, I'd only ever known people to say I love you to control me. My sperm donor used I love you as an excuse for why he hit me. Mom and Dad showed me they loved me, but it was just different when they said it. When he said it I was young; I panicked."

She takes a deep breath and looks at the ground. "By the time I realized, he had moved on and my heart shattered. I stayed away even longer. I came home for Megan's graduation and saw him. It killed me. I couldn't breathe. I knew I only had myself to blame. So, I left again. I took some time to get myself together, dated a few guys on the road, then Blaze met me at the Grand Canyon. We got the call that this place went up for sale and like I promised, I came back. By then, I'd learned how to live with it. But I haven't gotten over it."

"It can't be too late. Have you told him how you feel?" I ask

"No," she says and walks away.

I instantly feel him here.

Blaze.

I feel eyes on my back. I haven't heard a truck or anything pull up but a few seconds later, he's standing next to me at the fence, looking at Sage.

He glances over at me, and the heat of his stare is enough to make my knees go weak. No guy has been able to do that to me before.

"How's training going?" he asks me with a grin.

"Good. I can't wait to get in there with her, but she won't even let me think about it until I get the doctor's okay, even though I feel fine."

"Well, I have to back her on that one. The last week or so of a rib injury is tricky. You feel great, but it's the easiest time to re-injure when you do more than you should."

"Speaking from experience?" I ask.

"Yeah, broke a few ribs a few years back when my horse spooked. Re-broke them when I lifted more than I should have in the barn. I had felt fine. Then it took twice as long to heal. Mom and Sage wouldn't let me out of bed for a week." He grunts like he's annoyed, but I know he loves his mom and sister's attention.

"Yes, that sounds like Sage," I say.

"Have you thought any more about school?" he asks.

"Yeah, I don't know what I want to do. I love being out here with the horses, but I'm not sure if this is what I'm meant to do for the rest of my life. I don't want to take a blanket degree just to have one. I want something that specializes in what I want to do."

"Well, what are you interested in?" Sage asks, confirming she has been listening in all along while working the horse.

"I like history, particularly American history, but all the jobs I've looked into with history degrees are either boring or teaching, and I have no desire to teach. I applaud those who can, but I don't think I have what it takes to manage thirty-plus kids all day."

"Yeah, I don't blame you there," Blaze says.

"You know, if you like history, you really should check out the wagon tracks on Blaze's side of the ranch," Sage says as she looks at Blaze.

"Wagon tracks?" I ask

"Yeah from when people were heading west. Many who traveled on these tracks met up with the Oregon Trail," Blaze says.

I can tell my eyes light up. I've never had the chance to see anything like that in person. I have to see them.

"I'd love to see them!"

Sage looks over at Blaze. "Well, I'm tied down with the horses, but you should have Blaze take you tomorrow. You all can do lunch over there, and then he can show you some of the property. If you plan to stay here, you should see and know where some of the outlying cabins are. We use them if we get caught in weather on the far side of the ranch, or just need time away from everyone."

Oh, Sage is good. I have a feeling I know what she's doing. Blaze gives her a look but then looks over at me. "I'd be glad to take you tomorrow if you'd like?"

"I'd really like that," I say. I can barely stop myself from jumping up and down. I realize then that if Blaze is back, it must be close to lunchtime.

"Why don't I head in and get lunch going while you finish up?" I say to Sage.

"Sounds good." She gives me a wave.

"Need any help?" Blaze asks.

"Sure. If nothing else, I'd welcome the company." Wait, I would? Apparently, I would.

He smiles and walks inside with me.

Once inside, I pull everything out to make egg salad sandwiches. As I cook the eggs, Blaze clears his throat.

"If you're interested in horses, why don't you get an equine-concentrated degree?" he asks.

"What do you mean?"

"Well, there's a school out of Dallas that offers them. I believe it's all online. Sage looked into it at one point but decided to get something more to help run the ranch as a whole. I think there was a Bachelor of Science with an equine concentration, though that's more pre-med, vet related. There was also a Bachelor of Arts, with a business management in equine studies. That would cover more of what Sage does and allow you to work at any stable."

"I never thought of that. I guess I'll see how I do when I can actually get hands-on with the horse, but I like that idea."

"I think you'll do great with it." Blaze smiles at me as he toasts bread for the sandwiches.

I spend the rest of the day after lunch with Sage. She tells me it's girls' night. The guys are heading to their parents' house. Helen, Sage, Megan, and I are going to hang out at the house. Megan is going to do hair while the rest of us drink some wine, eat junk food, and gossip.

Sage's words.

So, after dinner, we all head our separate ways, and Megan sets up to cut my hair.

"Oooh, can I paint your nails?" Sage asks.

I shrug. "Sure." Knowing they won't last long on the ranch, but I don't want to dampen Sage's fun.

Helen is in the kitchen, making her famous brownies.

"Mom, you know you better be making a triple batch, or the guys will never forgive you!" Megan laughs.

"Oh, I am. They can have whatever we don't eat tonight," Helen replies.

"So, let's talk hair," Megan says. "Is this curl natural? Is the color natural? What were you thinking of doing? Please don't say bangs."

I laugh. "God, no bangs. I did that once in ninth grade. Let's just say I burned all the pictures. It was horrible!" Everyone laughs. "Yes, the curl in it is natural," I say of my loose, wavy hair. I am one of the lucky few to have natural beach waves everyone lusts after. A little product enhances it and makes my life easy.

"I'd kill for your hair," Sage says. I take in her brown locks.

"Trade ya?" I ask, and she laughs

"Gladly!"

"Also, yes, this is my natural color. It's been a year since I've had a haircut, so I know the dead ends need to be cut off. As for the rest of it, I was thinking Carrie Underwood circa 2012? The nice long hair with the face-framing and layers?"

Megan gets on her phone and types. "Like this?" She shows me a picture of Carrie at some red-carpet event. Her hair is stunning just like I'm picturing.

"Exactly like that!"

"I can do that. I think it will look great on you."

Megan sits me on a stool and gets to work. Sage has me pick out a nail color. I go with a pale pink. Helen finishes the first batch of brownies and hands me one with a glass of wine.

They talk about a cattle sale they're doing next month. Apparently, it's a big deal, and Helen has been planning a huge social event after the sale.

"The sale happens on Blaze's side of the ranch. We have a few horses up for sale this year too. There's a huge event space over there. We serve food, and there's music and drinks. It goes until late at night. It's a great way to make connections and bring in more horse business. I hope you'll be there. I'd like to show you off as a new part of the training business," Sage says.

"Are you sure? I've been keeping a low profile. I assumed you didn't want people to know I'm here," I say.

"Well, not for the reasons you're thinking. We were waiting to see if anything from your ex shows up, but it hasn't. We want to start introducing you to the town and get you settled in. The town is great. We have our gossips and a few bad apples, but they'll want to rally behind you. We figured once you were healed, there would be fewer questions. You can tell the story you want and not let your injuries speak for you."

I smile.

"We want people to know you are part of the ranch now," Helen says. "I hope you will, in time, think of us like family." She gives me a wide smile.

This woman has such a huge heart. She has already taken in three kids who had no one. Now, she doesn't bat an eye about wanting me to be part of her family. She reminds me so much of Mom.

"You guys want me to stick around? I always feel like I'm taking advantage because I don't have anything to offer in return."

Helen sits in front of me and takes my hand. "Riley dear, you'll learn something about us. What we give, we give freely with no expectations. You aren't taking advantage; we want you here. I can tell Sage has become attached to you. I think she's always needed another girl who has an idea of what she has been through to bond with."

"Moooomm," Sage says.

"Well, it's true, dear. And I won't pretend to see how you look at Blaze," Helen adds.

I feel my cheeks turn red.

"Oh, no need to be embarrassed," Sage says. "He looks at you the same way. While I know we're a bit biased, he's one of the good ones. That doesn't say he doesn't have his faults or moments, but in general, you couldn't pick a better guy."

My face must be as red as a tomato at this point, but Helen just smiles.

"She's right," Megan says. "And he's crazy protective of the people in his life. I had a boyfriend in high school talking about how long before he could get me to sleep with him. He was joking and taking bets from his buddies in the locker room. Blaze heard it all and beat the crap out of him. He got suspended for a week over it."

"Yeah, and he was treated like a prince at home for it," Helen says. "I was so proud."

"Really?" I ask.

"Of course! What mom wouldn't be proud that her son defended her daughter? He took care of Sage, never treated her differently because of it. He's always there for Megan, and his word is as good as gold. He never makes a promise he doesn't intend to keep."

"So, tell us a bit more about you," Sage says to me. "Tell us something we don't know."

"Umm, I had a twin who died at birth?" I say. Gruesome, I know, but it's a much safer topic than anything that could lead to Jed.

"I'm sorry to hear that, but of course, it does mean there's a chance you could have twins," Helen says with a glint in her eyes. I have to wonder if she's thinking of Blaze's twins running around.

"Okay, what do you think of your hair?" Megan asks as she hands me a mirror.

"Oh, I love it!!" I say and hug her. "Thank you!"

Then I have a thought and grab my hair tie and pull my hair up in a messy bun.

Megan's jaw drops. "Why..." she says.

I smile and blush. "Blaze is showing me the ranch tomorrow. I don't want him to see it until then," I say shyly.

There's a chorus of aww around the room.

"It's no big deal," I mumble, and Sage thankfully changes the topic.

We play twenty questions as Megan trims Sage and Helen's hair.

Then once Megan starts drinking, they break out the truth or dare. After a few rounds, they put on some music, and we all dance and drink. That's how the guys find us later that night.

We wrap it up and head to bed. I pass out the moment my head hits the pillow.

Chapter 9

Blaze

I'm wide awake, and my alarm hasn't even gone off yet. The sun is peeking through my window. There's no way I'm going back to sleep. Today's my date with Riley.

Okay, maybe it isn't a date. I want it to be a date, but having Sage push us together to show her the ranch probably doesn't qualify it as one.

Does it?

I'm praying it does.

I'm going to treat it like a date, which is why my nerves are on edge. I've been waiting for this for weeks. I was about to kill Sage when she suggested it, but then Riley said yes.

I'd wanted to hop the fence and hug my little sister but refrained.

Seeing her face light up when I mentioned the equine-specialized courses, I smiled like a fool for the rest of the day.

Then the girls had their night. Something about wine and hair. The guys and I ended up at my parents' house. We talked about the upcoming sale, drank some whiskey, and played cards.

Mom left us a batch of brownies, and I'm not ashamed to admit we ate them all. There were no survivors, and we have no regrets.

Then we headed back to the house to call it a night, and the girls had the music cranked up. Even Mom was dancing in the living room.

At first, I couldn't help but smile. This is what Sage has always wanted—a house full of family, loud and busy. Then I caught sight of Riley, and she took my breath away. She was smiling. A real smile that reached her eyes. They quickly kicked us upstairs, saying no guys allowed during girls' night, but they followed us by a half hour.

I pull myself out of bed and get ready for the day. Even though we're going to be around the ranch, I still put on something a bit nicer. I put on one of my nicer pairs of jeans and a dark gray button-down shirt and roll the sleeves up to my elbows. I pair it with my cowboy boots and my black cowboy hat.

I head downstairs and see I'm the first one there. No big surprise. I decide to make breakfast. I need to do something, and while I don't normally cook, I can cook well. Sage and Mom have made sure none of us guys got out of the house without knowing our way around the kitchen.

Jason and Mac are the first two downstairs, they give me a questioning look but don't say a word, thankfully.

Colt follows them a little later with a knowing smile.

"The girls are huddled in Sage's room. Giggles and music are coming from there. Should we be worried?" Colt asks.

"They're up to something. I suggest we get out of the house before they get downstairs," Jason says, and he and Mac finish their breakfast and bolt out the door.

Colt keeps looking at me and then asks, "You got a date with Riley, don't you?"

I can't help the grin that spreads across my face. "I don't know if it's a date. Sage pushed for me to show her the ranch and have lunch down by the wagon tracks."

"Well, show her you're date worthy. If it goes well, ask her out again. Something simple," Colt says.

"And I should take dating advice from the man whore of Texas why?"

"Because I do know women... normally," he mutters, and the girls come down the stairs. I see a look I can't quite make out, and he looks at Sage before walking out the door.

"Hey, you made breakfast," Sage says and turns to Riley. "This man can cook some mean omelets."

Riley comes into view and knocks me off my feet. She's wearing shorts with lace edging. She has a soft cream flowy shirt tucked into the front of her shorts with the back left untucked. It slips off her shoulder revealing her creamy skin. She has it paired with a leather bracelet set I know to be Sage's and a necklace and earring set I haven't seen before. She's wearing brown cowgirl boots, paired with one of Sage's brown cowgirl hats on her hand.

Then I notice her hair. Megan has done an amazing job; it frames her face in perfect loose waves.

"Riley, you look beautiful," I say, never taking my eyes off her. She blushes and tucks her hair behind her ear.

"Thanks. You look pretty good yourself," she says with a smile, and the thought of her checking me out has me getting hard.

No, think of breakfast; this isn't what today is about. My cock seems to have a mind of its own though, and it wants Riley.

Riley and Megan sit at the table, and I serve Riley a plate along with a cup of coffee made just the way she likes it.

"Thank you," she says.

"You're welcome, beautiful," I say and head back to make myself a plate and see Sage packing lunch for us with a smirk on her face.

I glare at her, and she just shakes her head.

As I sit back at the table, Megan has the same look on her face as Sage, and Colt looks like he has just been let in a huge secret.

"Well, some of us have to work today," Colt says, and he stands and smacks his hat on my shoulder. "Have fun." He grins the cheesiest smile before he walks out.

I mentally cross people off my Christmas list, starting with Colt. Bastard.

After Riley finishes, Sage tosses the sack of lunch toward me and pushes us out the door.

"I get the feeling she doesn't want us around for something, don't you?" I ask Riley.

"What made you think that? Her shoving us out the door or the look on her face?"

I laugh. "Both. I was thinking we could walk over to my side of the ranch to show it to you. Then we can take the ranch truck to the wagon trail. Is that okay?".

"Yes, that sounds great," she says.

We walk in silence until we hit the tree line, and I hold out my hand to help her over a fallen tree. She takes it and doesn't let go as we walk again. We head toward Mom and Dad's hand in hand.

"Hey, so I looked into that bachelor of arts program with an equine concentration you talked about," she breaks the quietness.

"Yeah, what did you think?" I ask.

"The program sounds amazing. Like you said, it can be done online. They want a certain amount of riding experience, but Sage said she and her business can sign off on it, so I can do that here at the ranch. I requested more info from them. I'm waiting on a packet in the mail," she says with a smile then quietly adds, "It will be my first piece of mail here at the ranch."

My heart soars at the thought of her settling in enough and getting mail at the ranch.

"That's awesome. This is your home now, so you should be getting mail," I say and squeeze her hand.

She talks a bit more about what she read on the program and then stops dead in her tracks.

"This is your parents' house?" she asks.

"Yes. While it looks a bit bigger, it's about the same size. Sage's is just a different layout," I say and direct her behind the house toward the event barn.

I give her a tour of the event space and then head toward the barn.

We run into Colt, and as soon as Riley sees him, she drops my hand. Colt smirks, and I glare at him.

"We're going to take the ranch truck," I tell Colt as I grab the keys and place my hand on the small of Riley's back to lead her toward the truck.

I open her door and help her in, placing the lunch sack from Sage in the backseat.

Now in the driver's seat, I head down the dirt path, heading back behind Mom and Dad's house. On the way, I explain how we use the different pastures. I point out the bunkhouse, and we talk a bit about the ranch hands.

Riley points out a footpath to our left.

"Where does that go?" she asks.

"To the family graveyard," I say and put the truck in park. "Want to go check it out?"

"Are you sure you don't mind?" she asks.

I hop out and come around to open her door. I hold her hand during the walk to the graveyard. I concentrate on how warm and soft her hand is and how perfectly it fits in mine. I worry that it's too much; I don't want to scare her off.

Then she shoulder checks me.

I look over and find her grinning. "Penny for your thoughts?" she asks.

"Sage and I say the same thing. I'm just happy to be showing you around. I was wondering what to show you next," I say. It isn't a complete lie.

We reach the graveyard, and I open the gate for her. She walks in and looks around.

"The older graves are in the back. In that back corner are my great-grandparents who settled here and built the first house. Their kids are buried along the back. Moving forward over here are my grandparents." I point toward the front left side of the row.

She looks around and takes it all in.

"So, your parents will be buried here?"

"Yes," I say, motioning toward the empty space in the front by the gate when we walked

THE COWBOY AND HIS RUNAWAY

in. There's plenty of room for my parents and even us kids.

"What happens when the graveyard is full?" she asks.

"Well, we'll just have to move the fence forward or to either side and make it bigger."

She smiles. "You plan to be buried here?" she asks.

"I do."

"And what about Sage, Colt, and Mac?"

"Well, they're as much a part of the family as I am, and they have a place here too. Though I guess we have to talk to Sage if she plans to be buried here or in her family graveyard on her side. My guess is she'll choose here to torment me for all of eternity."

Riley laughs. "I bet she would."

"Ready?" I hold my hand back out to her.

"Yes. I'm excited to see the rest of the ranch." She takes my hand. We head back to the truck and I open her door to help her in again.

I get in and pass the original cabin on the property, pointing to a few other homes we have as well.

"Ready to head out to the wagon trail?" I ask.

Her eyes light up. "Yes, I can't wait."

"I wish we could have taken the horses, but Sage would have buried me alive if I put you on a horse before talking to the doctor," I say.

"She's like the sister I never had. I love her to death, but she can be a bit much sometimes."

"It all comes from a good place. She saw what happened when I tried to do too much before I was cleared. I think she wants you safe because she's excited to get you working hands-on with the horses."

"I can't wait. Maybe next time we can take the horses out?" she asks.

She's already thinking of the next time. My heart swells.

"I'd like that," I say.

We come to a gate. "Do you want to slide over and drive the truck through? I'll get out and open the gate."

"Sure," she says and slides over to my seat as I get out. I open the gate and then close it behind the truck. I get back in, and she starts to slide back to the other side when I put my hand on her arm.

"You don't have to sit so far away, you know?" I say, trying to get her to sit next to me.

She looks at me with a look I can't quite make out.

"That depends on if this is a date, Blaze?" she asks bluntly.

I have no idea what to say but decide the truth is always the best way to go.

"Honestly, I don't know, but I'd like it to be." I watch her, worried it might scare her off. I can't blame her; the last guy she dated was a real tool.

Then she smiles. My breath catches, and she says, "I'd like it to be a date too." She nods and then gets comfortable in the middle of the bench seat.

Gone. I'm fucking gone for this girl. She's fucking amazing.

I can't wipe the smile off my face. As I drive, I hold her hand the whole way to the trail.

We hit the tree line, and I park the truck. "It's just beyond the trees. We have a short hike from here. You up for it?" I ask her.

"You bet I am," she says.

I take her hand again; I can't seem to keep my hands off her. It's like a drug I don't want to quit.

On the other side of the trees is a wide-open field and after walking for a few minutes, we come up on the trail.

"Oh, wow! This is amazing," she says.

Looking at it, it isn't much than some dirt ruts in the ground, but my family makes it a point to maintain it well. It's a piece of history, after all. We set out a blanket next to the trail while we eat the lunch Sage packed, I tell her all the history I know of the trail.

Riley asks about the history of the ranch, and I go over what I know about it as well.

"You guys are close to the Native Americans near here, right?" she asks.

"Yeah."

"They're the same tribe Mac comes from?" she asks like she's piecing together a puzzle.

"Yes, our family goes back many generations with the tribe," I tell her. I share some of the stories Dad told me growing up. She soaks it all in listening to every word I have to say.

I love that she wants to know so much about the ranch and the history here. I wish I knew more, but Dad has a journal with all the history in it in his office. Each generation adds to it.

She then asks about my past relationships. I tell her about my high school girlfriend and the girl I dated for a while after high school. There hasn't been anything serious since then.

She tells me about her high school boyfriend, her prom date, and then a bit about Jed. Riley shares how they met and how he was a good guy until he lost his job and started drinking. He got another job, and the drugs started. It got worse. She tells me about how she tried to leave a few times, but everyone in town didn't believe her about Jed. He was the town star quarterback, and everyone loved him. They kept taking her back to him, telling her to work it out. Then she seemed to clam up.

"Whenever you want to talk about Jed and everything, I'm here to listen. I'm not saying I'll like what I hear, but it's not good to keep it all bottled in. I'm always here to listen if you need to talk," I tell her.

"Thank you, but let's talk about something not quite as depressing," she says. "Tell me about this cattle sale."

So, I go into last year's sale and the people who will more than likely be there. I tell her to expect Mrs. Thompson to get shit drunk on the punch and not to eat Ed's 'special brownies' and to avoid Calvin. The more he drinks the more handsy he gets, even though he's completely harmless.

She laughs at the stories I tell her about people from the town.

We pack up and get back in the truck. I take a different route back home and show her some of the cabins on the far side of the ranch. I point out the creek that Sage and I got our 4-wheeler stuck in and tell her the story.

We head back to the barn behind Mom and Dad's house and park the truck. I help her out and ask her if she would like a tour. She accepts, and I take her in the back door.

Mom is standing in the kitchen when we walk in.

"Hey, Mom." I walk over and kiss Mom on the cheek.

She turns around and hugs me. "Hey baby, are you staying for dinner?"

"No, I just wanted to show Riley the house. Is that okay?" I ask.

"Of course, baby. Your dad is in his study. Make sure to say hi before you leave, okay? And Riley, I love your outfit! You look beautiful!"

"I promise, Mom." I turn to Riley. She thanks Mom, and I take her hand to show her the living room and dining room. We walk into the library, and she looks around wide eyed.

"Wow," she says.

"Yeah, this was Sage's favorite room growing up. Heck, it still is."

"I can see why. I'd never want to leave."

We then head down the hall to Dad's study. I peek my head in, and Riley and I say hello before we head upstairs. I show her Sage's old room, which hasn't been touched much since we moved out. It's bright and welcoming, filled with sunflowers.

"Can I see your room?" she asks a bit shyly.

"Sure." I shrug.

I open the door next to Sage's and step back, allowing her to take it in.

"Pirates of the Caribbean and Captain America?" she asks about the posters on the wall.

"Yeah well, it was better than the boy band crap Sage and Megan were obsessed with." I shrug.

"It's cute. Is it just Captain America or is it Avengers in general? Because I'm more of a Thor girl myself," she says.

I stare at her, amazed. She gets my nerdy side and even embraces it. This girl was made for me.

"All Avengers but of course you're a Thor fan." I laugh. "We will have to do an Avenger movie marathon sometime. Load up on popcorn and junk food."

"That sounds amazing."

"We better make our way home. I think Sage said something about making lasagna for dinner. Trust me, you don't want to miss that."

"Oh, that's my favorite!" she says.

We head downstairs to say goodbye to Mom and Dad and walk back to the house hand in hand.

"I had a really good time today," I say.

I watch her smile. "Me too."

"Would you be interested in doing this again, maybe dinner the day after tomorrow? We can take a picnic down to the creek. There's a great spot to watch a sunset down there," I ask her.

"I'd like that," she says, her eyes light up. "I'll make my Orange Crush cupcakes for dessert! I haven't made them in a long time. They're my favorite!"

I let out a breath I didn't realize I was holding and smile.

"Those sound amazing. You handle dessert, and I'll take care of the rest. Deal?"

"Deal," she says and skips the next couple of steps in excitement. I can't help but laugh.

When we reach the side door to the house, she starts up the steps, but I pull her hand back. She turns toward me and stops right in front of me. I take a deep breath and run my free hand up her arm. I gently move it to cup her cheek.

Take it slow, I remind myself. I see her look at my lips and then lick hers. Damn, she wants this as much as I do. I slowly lean in, giving her plenty of time to pull away if she doesn't want this. I drop her hand and put mine on her hip and pull her into me.

When my lips are just a breath away from her, I pause, making it very clear what I'm about to do. It's the most torturous few seconds of my life before I crash my lips on hers. She wraps her hands around my neck and pulls me in. I kiss her gently and move my hand from her cheek to the back of her neck to deepen the kiss. I lick the seam of her lips, asking for entrance. She parts her lips for me, and I take the moment to push my tongue past her lips. She leans into me, and I nip her bottom lip. She lets out the sexiest moan I've ever heard.

I pull back and kiss her gently on her lips then wrap her in a hug as I try to catch my breath. I feel her breathing as hard as I am, and I smile.

Then I remember we're standing by the back door and chuckle. "I can just see everyone crowded by the kitchen window, watching our every move," I say even though my back is to the window.

She peeks behind me and laughs. "Yep. Sage is going to corner me soon as I get in the house, isn't she?"

"She might wait until after dinner," I say. "I bet Mom called her to tell her we had just left her house and relay every detail. They're just as bad as the old biddies in town when it comes to gossip."

We laugh, and I take a deep breath. "Ready to head in?" I look her in the eyes and ask.

She nods, and I open the door for her. At least everyone has the decency to act like they had no idea what was going on just a minute ago.

"Dinner will be ready in thirty," Sage says.

"I'm going to go wash up then," Riley says and heads for the stairs.

"I'll join you," Sage says and wipes her hands on a kitchen towel.

"Sage," I growl. "Let her be."

"What, big brother? I haven't seen her all day. I can't talk to my friend and fill her in on what she missed with the horses?" she asks all smugly.

"We both know that's not what you're going up there to talk to her about."

She grins. "I have no idea what you're talking about," she says as she heads upstairs.

I sigh. Smiling to myself, I start planning dinner for our date.

Chapter 10

Riley

I go to close my bedroom door, and Sage catches it and pushes her way inside with a huge grin on her face. She flops down on the bed and says, "So, tell me everything."

"The trail was amazing. I had no idea there was so much history here. Blaze said your dad has a journal with the history of the land? Do you think I could read it sometime?"

She waves her hand. "Of course, but that's not what I want to know. I know the history; tell me about Blaze!"

"This isn't weird? He's your brother, after all," I say.

She shrugs her shoulders. "Trust me, when you're talking about the details, I'm NOT picturing Blaze in my head. I have my own hottie to drool over."

"Are you ever going to tell me who it is?" I ask.

"Maybe, but not right now. Now stop stalling and talk."

I laugh. "Well, he gave me a tour of the ranch. We saw his family's graveyard, some of the cabins, and then we had lunch. We talked about the ranch and the reservation. We talked about his past relationships and mine. I told him a bit about Jed, not a lot. He told me some stories from when you guys were kids."

Sage cringes. "Nothing too embarrassing, I hope?"

"No, just some funny ones. We stopped in and saw your mom and dad. He gave me a tour of the house. I might have drooled a bit too much over the library!"

"Did he show you his old room?"

"Yes, and yours."

"What did you think?"

"I teased him about Captain America since I'm a Thor girl myself. We talked about an Avengers movie marathon."

"God, you really are the perfect girl for him."

I laugh. "Then we came back here." I shrug my shoulders.

"And..."

"And what?" I try to play dumb.

"Oh, come on. They saw sparks from that kiss from space! It was hot!"

"I knew you were watching from the window!"

"Damn straight, I was. I had to make sure my brother treated my friend right." She laughs. "But come on, give me something. Was it a good kiss?"

"It was the best kiss of my life."

"Yes! So, do you have another date planned?"

"Yes, day after tomorrow. He said a picnic dinner down by the creek. I offered to make dessert, He's going to take care of the rest."

"Oh, any idea what you're going to make?"

"Yes, my Orange Crush cupcakes. I haven't made them in forever. They're my favorite!"

"Please say you'll make enough for us here at the house too!"

"Of course, but I need to head to town to get what I need."

"Well, I have a running grocery list. We can go into town tomorrow and grab everything. Sound good?"

"Perfect!"

"I need to check on dinner. It should be almost done. I'm so happy for you guys!"

"Thanks."

After she's left, I flop on the bed and the day runs through my head.

I have a date.

With Blaze.

I have a date with Blaze.

Wow. I'm never that blunt where it comes to asking him if it was a date. Around him, I have this whole new confidence. I like it, and I'm terrified at the same time.

I get ready for dinner thinking about our next date.

• • • • • • • • • •

The next morning, I stand in the kitchen staring out the kitchen window, watching Blaze and Colt walk into the barn. Well, let's be honest, my eyes haven't moved off Blaze's back end. Come on, he has a nice butt. There's something about a cowboy in wranglers that can make a girl swoon.

"Nice view, huh?" Sage comes up next to me, staring out the window. She has a look of sadness on her face, but it disappears before I can ask any questions.

"Ready to head into town?" Sage asks.

"Yes, let's do it."

"If you're up for it, I thought we'd grab lunch at the café. Talk to some of the girls in town. Maybe stop by the beauty shop and let people get to know you?"

"Yeah, I'm okay with that, as long as you're sure it's safe. Wait, the beauty shop?"

Sage chuckles. "Yeah, when you want to gossip, go straight to the source. The girls at Megan's always have the latest news and spread it fast. They're the quickest way to get the town to know and love you. But be warned, they already know the basics of your story. Megan made sure the truth was passed around so they would protect you if anyone came asking. "

I instantly become a bit more nervous, but Sage seems to notice and wraps me in a quick hug.

"I promise not to leave your side. I'll save you from the twenty questions everyone will want to play," Sage says.

I take a deep breath and force a smile. "Okay, let's go."

We get in Sage's truck and head out the main gate.

Sage looks like she's concentrating on something, so I give her a few minutes to work through it before I break the silence.

"It's Colt, isn't it?" I ask.

She looks startled and then sighs. "How did you guess?"

"I've been watching you two in the last few weeks. Do the guys know?"

"NO! And you can't tell them. *Especially* Blaze. If anything comes of it, *I* need to be the one to tell him."

"I understand and promise I won't say a thing. Now spill, so I can help."

Sage laughs and spends the rest of the drive into town giving me the short version of how she and Colt fell for each other. When he said he loved her, she panicked and left to travel. She admits to going about it all wrong and how she left.

After she left, Blaze told her that Colt started drinking and sleeping around, which stopped her from coming home sooner. She shares how much it hurts seeing him do it now, but he's a lot tamer now that she's back. But it's still a knife in the gut.

We pull into the café parking lot, and she turns to face me. "I don't think I could take it if he said I missed my chance and turned me down. To live here for the rest of my life and watch him with someone else, I can't do it."

"Sounds like the thought of you with someone else is what put him in this place.

What would it do to him to see you with someone else?" I ask.

She doesn't say anything, just stares over my shoulder in silence. "Are you suggesting I date and give him a taste of his own medicine?" she finally asks.

I shrug my shoulders. "I'm the last one to give dating advice, but I'm always here to talk things out. My advice may suck, but I'll give it freely."

She finally smiles. "I have nothing to lose at this point. Maybe I need a date for this sale coming up. What do you think?"

I smile back. "Let's get you a date!"

As we head into the café, I notice a new spring in her step. It may not work, but at least she has a plan of action now. That seems to be all she needs to perk up her mood.

This is the same café and feed store Lilly dropped me off at the night we pulled into town. I shake the thought from my head. Things are going well; don't invent trouble that hasn't found you yet. That's what my momma used to say.

You know in the movies when the character walks into a room and everyone stops talking and turns to look at you? Yeah, that totally happens when I walk into the café with Sage. I'm not kidding one bit.

Sage looks at me, rolls her eyes, and grabs my hand like she's afraid I'll bolt. She's totally right on that; the thought crosses my mind.

"Guys, this is Riley. She's new to town. Don't pretend you don't know her story. I warned her about all of you. If you don't treat her right, you'll answer to me and my family. Got it?" Sage says in a louder voice than I've heard from her.

My face heats up. I don't like being the center of attention. I watch as everyone looks at me; some smile, some show no expression. Within a few seconds, they all turn back to their food and their conversations like it never happened. Though now, I'm ninety-nine per cent sure every conversation is about me.

Sage pulls me along to a booth in the back corner near a window.

"Ignore them all. Some new gossip will come along in a few days, and you'll just be another member of the town. Trust me, I know it sucks. I've been the center of the gossip more than once. I even left town to get away, but it follows you. Now, let's eat and scout dates."

I laugh and look at the menu. Lots of Southern good-old diner food.

"How you girls doing today?" A woman in her forties with curly golden-blond, shoulder-length hair and rectangle black-rimmed glasses comes over. She's smiling as she looks at Sage and then me.

"Hey, Jo, how are you?" Sage asks the woman.

"I'm good. Been busy as always. Riley, hun, don't let them get to you. We're so happy you're here. If you need anything, you just let me know, okay?"

A bit stunned, I barely mumble out a thank you.

"Now, what can I get you, ladies, to eat? It's on the house today to welcome Riley here to town."

"Oh, you don't have to do that," I say.

"I know I don't, but I want to," Jo says with a smile.

"Don't fight her. You won't win," Sage says with a smile.

We both get the fried chicken platter and sweet tea. Sage fills me in on who's who like I'm ever going to remember all these names. Many people come in for to-go orders, and I notice several checking Sage out. She seems to either not notice or ignore them.

"So, any thoughts on the date?" I ask Sage.

She gives me a tight-lipped smile. "I guess any of the guys will do, but none hold any appeal."

"Well, there's one more option. You could tell Mac what's going on and have him be your date. It would amp up the jealousy factor and no hard feelings because he'd be in on the ploy," I say.

She laughs. "Before you, I would have just confided in Blaze and asked him to do it, and he would have. Jason is too old fashion for that, so it leaves some guy from town or Mac. Lovely. Let me think about it."

"Think about what, baby doll?" Jo asks as she drops off our food.

"Well, I need a date for the sale."

"Oh honey, you can't throw a stone in this town without hitting a guy who would love to date you. We all figure you'll land with either Blaze or Colt, so no one tries." She pats Sage's arm and walks away.

We finish our lunch, keeping the topics light. I can tell Sage is in deep thought and figure it's best to let her process.

After lunch, we head to the store to shop, figuring that after the show at the café we can skip the beauty shop today. I'm happy to agree with that.

After we get home, I take over to make dinner. The café has me craving Mom's meatloaf.

I'm just putting the meatloaf in the oven when the skin on the back of my neck prickles. I can tell Blaze's eyes are on me. I hadn't heard him come in, but then again, I'm lost in thought on how I can help Sage.

I turn around, and his eyes meet mine. Neither of us move, but there's a sizzle in the air. It's intense.

When Blaze finally speaks his voice is a bit hoarse. "Dinner smells amazing. What can I help with, beautiful?"

I smile at him. A man in the kitchen isn't something I'm used to.

"Well, everything's pretty much set, so you can just keep me company," I say as I sit on the stool next to him.

We talk about the day, minus anything about Colt and Sage looking for a date. He tells me about his work on the ranch and plans for the next few weeks. I tell him about the way Sage introduced me to the café, and I try to remember the names of a few people we ran into at the store.

It's all very relaxed and domestic, something I've always pictured doing with my husband.

Whoa.

Stop rewind.

What?

Husband.

No.

We've had one date!

Chapter 11

Blaze

Sage and I get to talking with the guys about the plans for the sale. By the time we get upstairs and check on Riley, she's passed out in her own bed.

I head into Sage's room. "Riley is asleep in the bed in the guest room," I say.

Sage smiles. "You mean her bed in her room?"

I grunt in response because I know she's right.

"That's good though, I want to talk to you," Sage says as she sits on the couch.

"Please skip the birds and the bees talk. Mom beat you to it many years ago."

Sage gives a small laugh. "No, it's about me."

I sit next to her and turn to face her. I can see she's been thinking.

"I think I want to take a date for the sale. But I'm pretty sure you guys have scared off anyone in a hundred-mile radius," she says.

"Well, tell me who you want to go with, and I'll scare them back into taking you," I joke.

She laughs. "I honestly don't know. I just don't want to go alone."

"What about Brice? Remember him from school? We stayed friends, and he's always had a crush on you. He's a good guy, and I know I can take him if I need to," I say with a smile.

Sage shakes her head. "I always liked Brice. What's he doing now?"

"He helps his dad over at the doctor's office now."

"Wait, he became a doctor?" Sage asks, shocked. I guess I didn't realize how much she didn't keep in touch with people other than us after she left.

"Yeah, he does a lot of the house calls now so his dad can work the clinic. He built a house on the property in town over by the clinic and is doing pretty well."

"Hmm, maybe you can speak to him for me? Tell him you won't kick his ass for asking me out, and that I'm interested?"

"Of course, I'm heading down that way later this week to settle our account. I'll try to catch him then."

She looks like she still has something else on her mind.

"Okay, spill it. You have something else to talk about. It's written all over your face."

"Just worried a bit. We haven't heard anything from that Jed guy. I want this all to be over with."

I look at Sage, really look at her, I can tell this isn't what's bothering her, but I know her. She'll tell me when she's ready, I just have to let her work through it.

"Me too, but we'll handle it when the times comes. I hate the idea of Riley feeling like she has to look over her shoulder for the rest of her life."

Sage lays her head in my lap just like we used to, and we watch some TV. A habit she has stopped since Riley has been around. A sign she really likes Riley.

As we head to bed, I stop Sage.

"Will you head down and stay with Riley in her room, please? I still don't want her sleeping alone."

"Blaze, she's fine. The alarm is set, and she obviously wants some space."

"Hey, you're to blame, bringing up Jed and all earlier. Now, it's on my mind. If you don't, I will."

I hear her cuss under her breath, but she grabs her phone charger and gun and heads into Riley's room. I breathe a little easier knowing she's with her.

· · · ● ● · ● ● · ·

The next morning, I wake up with thoughts of our date that evening on my mind. I get ready for the day and head downstairs to find only Sage. Perfect.

I ask her to make sure Riley is ready by five p.m. She agrees and has a hint of amusement in her eyes when I refuse to tell her my plans.

Next, I head over to Mom and Dad's place. They're up early most days. Mom is in the kitchen and makes me a cup of coffee before sitting to talk to me.

I tell her my plans but ask her to fix me something that I can store in a cooler just in case things don't work out. She agrees, and I kiss her before heading to my office in a sad attempt to get some work done.

My mind is always on Riley, and I wish I could text her, but she doesn't have a phone. I make a mental note to look at adding her to my phone plan.

After lunch, I head out to get things set up for our date. I want to have a good-old country date and see how well she fits into my life. This is always a good test, the girls who don't do well on the country date are never around long.

At the same time, I want this date to be different from any others; Riley is special. I feel it in my gut, she's one of those rare people that come into your life when you least expect it and toss your world upside down in the best possible way. I plan to hold on and keep her in my life if she'll let me.

I notice it's time for me to get ready. I choose to shower at Mom and Dad's and get ready there, so I can pick her up like a true date. I then head out to Mom's garden to pick some fresh flowers for her. As I look around, I realize I have no idea what her favorite flower is. Crap.

Mom must see me standing there because she comes out and loops her arm in mine and takes me toward the back of the garden. "She has a boho, country style, baby. Go with wildflowers. A mixture of colors."

I have no idea what she means by her style, but I trust Mom, and we put together a mixture of oranges, pinks, and purples that go well together. Mom then ties them together with a ribbon and hands me a cooler for tonight. I thank her and place both in my truck and make sure I have everything else I need in the back before I head over to the house to pick up Riley.

I decide to go all out and walk up to the front door and ring the doorbell. A moment later, Sage answers with a gun in hand.

"What in the devil are you doing?" she asks.

"I'm here to pick up Riley for dinner," I say.

We smile, and Sage shakes her head. "And what are your intentions with my daughter?" Sage jokes, but I can't answer her because Riley is coming down the stairs, and I can't breathe.

She's wearing an off-white lace dress that stops just below her knees with brown cowboy boots and a matching brown belt. She has on a short jean jacket that ends at her waist with earrings and a hair clip the same blue as the jacket. She has a brown purse, the same color as the boots, and a brown cowgirl hat as well.

I step forward into the doorway just as she reaches the bottom of the stairs.

"You're breathtaking, Riley," I say and notice the slight blush that crosses her cheeks.

"So are you, Blaze," she says, and I catch her eyes running down my body. I'm in an outfit like our last date. Dress jeans with a blue button-down shirt this time, my black cowboy hat, and boots.

Riley stops in the kitchen and grabs a Tupperware container then makes her way over to me.

"Dessert," she says and smiles. I take her hand and look at Sage who's watching with a dreamy look in her eyes.

We head out to my truck and I help Riley buckle in, before heading to my side of the truck. I take a deep breath and climb in.

I'm a bit nervous about this date. I need to make sure she fits into the ranch. She already gets along great with everyone including Sage. That's important. I've had girls get jealous over my friendship with Sage, and that's a deal breaker.

Sage isn't going anywhere; she's family and more than that, she's my best friend. The only girl who will know me better than her will be my wife. If I'm being honest, when I picture my wife, I see Riley in that spot. That both excites me and scares me at the same time.

I head down the driveway to the main road, showing her how secure the driveway is. I head down the road a bit to another gate that looks like the last one. I punch in my code and drive in.

"This is still our property," I say. "This was the only driveway to my parents' house. We made the other one when we bought the land Sage's house is on. It actually makes the drive to my parents' shorter and makes this church here private."

I pull in front of a small church. "My family that settled this land built this church for a few of the ranch families in the area. We maintain it and while it isn't used weekly now, we have an event or two here every now and then. It's used for family weddings and funerals."

"It's beautiful," she says, staring at the small church. There's a door in the center and a window on each side. It's small but above the door is an old stained-glass circle window that's original to the church from the 1800s.

After a bit, we keep driving and take a fork in the road to the right. We're driving down a ranch road that separates our field when we get to a tree line. I drive along the tree line for a little bit before stopping.

Riley looks over at me and smiles. I walk over and help her out of the truck then grab a few things from the back. Riley has her Tupperware, and we walk through the trees to a large creek that runs down this side of the property.

"So, I thought a good-old country date would be in order," I say and watch her as she smiles.

"What did you have in mind?" she asks.

I set my stuff down, spread out the blanket, and set the cooler on it.

"I'm thinking we catch our dinner in the creek and then have a nice picnic and go from there?"

"Oh, I haven't been fishing since my dad died. I used to love going to the lake with him!"

She's excited about the date, which makes me excited. We get our poles set up and as we stand at the side of the creek, Riley talks about fishing with her dad and catching her first fish and how.

As we talk, Riley gets a tug on her line and catches a small bass. She has no problems taking it off the hook herself, and I take a picture of her holding it with my phone. We add it to the cooler and decide to try for one more fish for dinner.

We talk about me growing up on the ranch and how I handled Sage leaving for a bit and my trip with her to the Grand Canyon when I get a tug on my line, catching another bass. I make a small fire and set to cooking the fish in the breading Mom gave me.

Once ready, I pull out some cornbread and rice from the cooler and a bottle of wine. We have a great dinner, eating and talking.

Chapter 12

Riley

Talking to anyone, much less a guy, has never been as easy as it is with Blaze. We sit by the creek and talk until the sun goes down. Then we pick up and head back to his truck where he spreads out the blanket in the back and pulls out a few pillows from the backseat. As we lie on the bed of his truck we watch the stars and talk.

I have my head on Blaze's shoulder, and I'm pressed up against his side. His arm behind me is lightly running up and down my spine. I can't remember the last time I've been in someone's arms so lovingly.

Right now, there's a break in the conversation, but it's not uncomfortable. Being here with each other is enough. I can't remember ever having that before.

I decide it's time to open up to Blaze. He's a good man, not only can I tell, but people vouch for him. I know Sage won't put up with any crap after what she's been through. The other night, she showed me a photo album of her injuries when she filed her police report. She was banged up worse than me.

She has told me she'll always protect me, and the guys here will too. I guess my gut knows it but hearing it is something else. Then she has told me how Blaze was there for her and all he's been through because of her.

She then turns to me and says, "Blaze is one of the best guys. He's my best friend and my brother. He really likes you, and I think you two would be good together. Don't let what Jed did hold you back, but don't rush into it either. When you're ready to move forward, you have to open up to him and tell him everything. You don't have to tell us, though I hope one day you will. If you want a future with Blaze, you have to tell him."

I've spent several nights thinking about that, and I know it's time. I can see a future here with Blaze. This place feels like home for the first time since my parents' ranch. When I see my future, I see horse training with Sage and a family with Blaze.

I roll over onto my back, keeping my head on Blaze's shoulder, and take a deep breath.

"When my parents died, I went to live with my aunt, my mom's sister. She was the only family I had left, but she wasn't a real family. She never wanted kids, and my mom never got along with her. From the bits and pieces I've heard over the years, I guess my aunt was in love with my dad and was pissed he chose my mom."

Blaze runs his thumb up and down my arm, and it allows me to go on.

"When I went to live with my aunt, she didn't want me. I was a reminder of the man who didn't want her, and she treated me as such. I was often ignored. I had to fend for myself. She never bought me clothes or made me dinner. So soon as I could, I got a job. Then she charged me rent, so I couldn't save up any money.

"The day I turned eighteen, I came home from school to my bags on the front porch and a note saying I wasn't her problem anymore and to not come back. I was a few weeks from graduating and had nowhere to go. A friend snuck me into her room for a few weeks each night after her parents went to bed, so I had someplace to sleep and shower. When she went away early to college a few days after graduation that ended.

"I was waiting tables at the diner, and Jed had been coming in once a week or so. Once I graduated from school, it was more regular. He was a few years older than me and was the high school quarterback but tore his ACL. He stayed home and went to school online to help his mom who had cancer. His dad had died a few years before, and the town just fawned over him. He gave me his attention.

"He never pushed. He just came in three times a week, sat in my section, and asked questions about how I was doing, my plans, and my dreams. All that stuff you talk about when you're dating. He always left a twenty-dollar tip on a bill that was around ten dollars. One night, I worked the late shift, and he was in for dinner. It was the first time I was closing, and there had been a break-in at a store a few buildings down earlier in the week. Jed stayed in the café and said he'd walk me out to make sure I was okay.

I take a deep breath. "I was scared. I didn't have anywhere to go. I'd been cleaning up at work and eating there too. I slept on a bench at the park one night, in an empty house for a while too. When Jed found out, he got mad at the situation. He kept saying he wished he knew so he could have taken care of me. He insisted I stay at his place until I got on my feet. He had an extra bedroom. The girl I waitressed with encouraged me to do it, so I did.

"He lived in a trailer on his family's land a few minutes outside town. He said he'd give me rides to work. He was still a perfect gentleman. He refused to allow me to pay rent but said I could cook and clean the house if I felt up to it. So, I did. When I worked nights, I would have something in the fridge for him to warm up, and I'd make breakfast. When I was home for dinner, I cooked."

I shift a bit closer to Blaze then and with his hand not rubbing my arm, he holds my hand.

"Well for a while, things were good. He worked and would bring me home some things, saying he thought about me. He bought me a cell phone, so I could talk to him when he was at work or when I was on my break. I look back now and things I thought were romantic, it should have been red flags. Later, he used the phone to track me. He would suggest date nights mostly at home instead of going out with friends. Then one day, he came in for dinner while I was working a dinner shift, and a guy we'd never seen came in. He looked like a trucker passing through.

He sat down and flirted with me, and Jed lost it. He kicked the guy out and took me home, ranting the whole way how my boss flirts with me and now this guy.

"He apologized as soon as we got home. He said he was jealous and wasn't thinking. He told me that night he loved me. He asked me about quitting my job and going to school online full time. He said he'd pay for it. He wanted me to focus and get a good education. He'd done so much for me, I wanted to make him happy. But this was his final way of isolating me. A week after I quit my job, he claimed to start the process of getting me enrolled. He set me up for SAT testing, which we had to wait two weeks for me to take. After that, he said he had to wait on my transcripts. That was another two weeks. Then he had to wait on the forms in the mail. He dragged it on for two months. Then his mom died.

"That was when he lost it. He started drinking, and I thought he was just grieving. I know what it's like to lose your parents, so I took care of him. A month later, he lost his job. He kept showing up drunk. Then the house was never clean enough, the food never good enough. He tried to get another job. After the fifth time, he was turned down, I offered to look over his resume. We could do a mock interview to see if I could help him. He told me he didn't need help and backhanded me, busting my lip."

Blaze tenses and I squeeze his hand.

"I was in shock, so I ran and locked myself in the bathroom. He immediately apologized, and I fell asleep crying. He fell asleep apologizing right outside the door. So, I forgave him. He stopped drinking during the day, and he got another job, but he would go from his job to the bar and come home drunk and high. When he was drunk, he would throw things and yell. When he was sober, he apologized and was the sweet man I fell in love with. The man the town knew.

"One day, I was out at the grocery store. I went weekly to buy groceries with the little money he gave me, so I budgeted down to the penny. I even took a calculator with me and a list. I think it would take me two hours to max the budget right, but I enjoyed it. The grocery store was across the street from the bar. I had the car, and he said he'd get a ride home with a friend. I saw him fall into the backseat of a car, making out with a blonde. Didn't take a genius to figure out what happened next."

At this point, I roll over, facing Blaze, and press up against his side for comfort.

"I went home, unloaded the groceries, packed a bag, and waited. I wanted to confront him. I wanted him to know I saw him. Looking back, I should have just run. It would have been the perfect timing. I didn't know then that he had lost his job again. But when I got home and confronted him, he lost it. He told me if I wasn't such a prude and opened my legs more, he wouldn't have to find it elsewhere. He blamed me for his drinking and losing his job. He hit me again and when I fell, he kicked me and told me to clean the bathroom. So, I did.

"He never went for another job after that. He stayed home drank and if I spoke about it, I got beaten. I guess the only saving grace was he never tried to rape me. There's the bright side, right? A few weeks later, I got a break to run. He went to the bar, I guess to find another girl. I ran into town, right to the police station. I showed them the healing bruises, and they brought Jed in. I don't know what was said but from what I know, he told them I fell down the front stairs while shaking out a rug. I had been making up wild stories about seeing UFOs in the sky at night. He said he loved me and wanted to help me, so they handed me right back over to him! They believed him because he was the town golden boy, and I was the orphan who had no one."

Blaze pulls me closer and kisses the top of my head like he knows what's coming.

"That night, I got the worst beating I had until that point. I couldn't move for at least a week. I'm pretty sure he broke a rib or two. So, I thought that my friends at the diner would help me. So, when I got another break a month later, that's where I went. I had a busted lip and bruises on my arms then, but my aunt was there and she'd heard from the sheriff so she called Jed. She painted me a crazy person, and everyone looked at me like I was when he picked me up. He was all sweet and loving, and he put on a good show. When we got home though, he almost killed me that night. I remember going in and out of consciousness for days, and he was pissed about it, so he beat me again."

"Riley..." Blaze says, his voice raw. I can't look at him yet.

"So, I knew I had to run. I bid my time, telling him what he wanted to hear, doing what he wanted. I healed. I took ten dollars from his wallet one night and waited until he went to the bar again. I snuck out and went to the store to buy sleeping pills. I came home and hid them. A few days later, I crushed one up and put it in one of his nighttime drinks. He slept, but it didn't knock him out. He stirred at every sound. He woke up that night and wailed into me. The sleep meds made him crazier. So, the next night, I crushed up three times the dosage and mixed it between two of his drinks. He passed out cold and crumpled to the floor. I made sure he was alive then took the money from his wallet. Forty dollars, and I ran."

Lost in thought, I pause for a moment. Blaze squeezes my shoulder, pulling me out of my thoughts.

"This time, I ran to the highway. I planned to hitchhike. I figured any trucker had to be better than Jed. I got lucky. The trucker who picked up was a woman named Lilly. She was the nicest person I had met in a long time. I lied that I had a friend outside Dallas that I could call once we got to her stop. I figured I could just lay low then hitchhike again. I wanted out of Texas. She bought me food and since she traveled at night, I got a good night's sleep. She got me some painkillers, and her next stop was at the feed store here in town. I told her I would stay at the bed and breakfast and call my friend. She gave me her number and said goodbye.

"I saw the bar and was hungry. I decided I might get lucky and find a takeout box someone forgot in the trash, and I did. I was trying to plan my next move when two guys stumbled out, yelling and fighting. I knew I had to hide, so I got in the back of a truck that had some blankets and covered up. I guess I fell asleep. The next thing I knew, the truck started, and I ended up here. I climbed into the barn, intent on resting. Then you found me."

Blaze is quiet for a minute before speaking. "I'm so glad you ended up here, and I'm glad you told me. I promise you; he'll never hurt you again. I take care of what is mine and Riley, beautiful, I want you to be mine."

I have tears in my eyes when I look up at Blaze. "That's why I told you. I want to be yours too."

He wipes away my tears with his thumbs then leans in and kisses me soft and sweet. "Good, because I'm yours," he whispers against my lips before kissing me again. I wrap my arms around his neck and pull him down to me as I roll onto my back.

Blaze braces himself on his arms over me to not crush me but never breaks the kiss. I don't know how long we kiss for—minutes, hours, days, but when we pull apart, we're breathing heavily. Blaze looks into my eyes, and I stare right back.

There are no words to complete this moment, so I just pull him back and keep kissing him. I've never felt like this with anyone, not even Jed at the beginning. I feel safe and protected, loved, and cherished, special, and free to be me.

I shift under Blaze, my hips lifting and rubbing against his rock-hard cock under his jeans, making him groan. Then he grinds into me, hitting my clit, making me gasp and moan.

Blaze pulls away and looks into my eyes and grinds into me again, watching my face. My back arches to meet his hips this time.

"We can stop anytime, Riley. You set the pace," he whispers.

I shake my head. "Don't stop," I gasp as he grinds into me again.

He kisses down my neck, and his hand trails down my side, stopping at my hip and pulling me closer to him while he adjusts his angle.

He buries his face into my neck and groans. I scratch my nails up and down his back.

Every time his cock hits my clit, it sends shockwaves across my body that pulls the tension cord shorter. The pleasure builds up faster than ever before.

"So close," I gasp as Blaze takes my mouth again and then grinds down hard and fast, causing me to explode and scream his name. When my body stops convulsing, I look up and see he's watching me and breathing hard.

"I've never seen anything so sexy. You're beautiful. Thank you for giving yourself to me like that," he says and leans down to kiss me. He rolls to the side and gathers me in his arms.

I rest my head on his shoulder and notice he's still hard. I reach down and grab his cock over his jeans, and he groans and grabs my hand.

"Not tonight, beautiful. Tonight is about you. You set the pace, and we'll go slow."

"But don't you want to come too?" I ask, knowing my face has to be bright red.

"God, yes, but watching you come undone, that's all I need. I'll take care of him later." He shifts, pulling me close. "Lie with me a bit longer before we head back."

Later that night, Blaze walks me upstairs and kisses me good night. "You go crawl in bed with Sage, okay?" he asks.

I nod, and he kisses me again before heading to his room. I can't remember a more perfect night.

Chapter 13

Blaze

It's been a week since my dinner with Riley down by the creek. We've spent time together every night, even if it's just watching TV in her room or sneaking away for an hour for lunch.

After Riley opened up to me about Jed, it's like the last wall between us is gone. I love how she trusts me and how carefree she is. It takes everything in me to not hunt this Jed guy down and kill him, but I can't stand the thought of anything taking me away from Riley.

Riley has sent her application into the school to enroll, so we're now just waiting to hear back. She has been taking well to the horses and training with Sage, who says she's a natural and is excited to have her.

Today, I head to town to talk to Brice for Sage and run a few errands. My first stop is the clinic and thankfully, Brice is in.

"Hey Blaze, how's it going?" Brice greets me.

"Good, man, how're things going here at the clinic?" I ask.

"Going good. What can I help you with?"

"Well, I'm here for a non-doctor reason, you got a minute?"

"Sure, want to head into my office?"

"Yeah, that would be great."

Once there and seated, I just dive right in.

"Are you seeing anyone right now?"

He laughs "No, but, Blaze, you aren't my type," he jokes.

I laugh and shake my head.

"Sage is looking for a date to the sale in a few weeks. She knows the guys and I've scared off pretty much everyone, so she sent me here."

I watch him sit up straighter. "Sage is looking to date? Rumor has it she hasn't been interested since she came home."

I nod. "She hasn't. With getting the ranch up and going, I don't think she's had time. But Riley and I have been dating, and she's been watching. I think she's just ready now. I know you had an interest in her before, and I know you're a good guy. All I'm saying is if you're still interested, I approve and won't stand in your way."

He watches me for a bit then smiles. "I've always had a bit of a crush on Sage. She has just been that girl that was untouchable, ya know?"

I nod. I know Colt and I basically threatened everyone and anyone who looked her way growing up.

"Well, if you're interested, swing by the ranch this week and ask her to dinner. She has a few horses she's training with Riley, so I don't think she'll be in town this week."

He nods and smiles. "I'll do that. Is she still the simple, what you see is what you get, kind of girl?"

I nod. "She is, but the warning stands. Treat her right or deal with all four of us. Got it?"

"I wouldn't expect anything else." He stands and shakes my hand.

I head out and run some errands. I'm at the feed store when Shane the town sheriff walks in.

"Blaze, I need a word if you can swing by the station soon as you're done here?"

I nod. Shane is a family friend and a good guy, but I have this knot of dread in the pit of my stomach over this talk.

When I finish up at the feed store, I walk down to the sheriff's office and am ushered right in. He closes the door.

"I was about to head out to your place but heard you were in town. Thought I'd grab you first. Listen, Jed put out a missing person report on Riley."

I feel the blood drain from my face.

"That means if someone picks her up, they'd take her to the station back where he filed."

"They would turn her over? She went to the police there, and they handed her back to Jed. They didn't help her." I feel my voice rising.

"Blaze, son, I'm on your side here. We need Riley to come down, answer the report, and make a statement that she isn't missing. Now, she has to file a report on Jed because he'll know where she is."

My blood runs cold.

"Blaze, it has to be today."

I nod. "Okay, let me call Sage. She can bring her in."

I get ahold of Sage and explain the situation. I talk to Riley, and she agrees to file, but she's panicking. I can tell. I tell Sage to bring Colt with them, just in case.

An hour later, we're sitting back in Shane's office when she gives a statement against the missing person's report. Sage and Colt wait outside while Riley files her report against Jed with the doctor's files from the day she arrived and his findings on the old fractures that match her story.

She tells him everything, down to the police not helping and sending her back down, to her drugging him to get away. All with tears pouring down her face.

"What happens now?" I ask.

"Well, because the report will also be against the deputy there who didn't help her, a state police officer will head in to detain Jed. I'm taking this to a judge, and you'll have a restraining order within twenty-four hours, but Jed could make bail. You need to be aware, and I suggest staying on the ranch. Your address won't be posted, but he can likely find out you're in Rock Springs and head this way."

Riley is white as a ghost.

"That's only if he makes bail," Shane says. "I'll personally follow this and let you know what happens. You have my number if you need me."

We take Riley home, and Colt goes to tell Mom and Dad what happened. He tightens up security while Sage tells Mac and Jason, who tightens patrol around the grounds on our side. After dinner, the sheriff comes to visit.

"Here's your restraining order, but like I tell my daughters, it's just a piece of paper. Don't let your guard down."

Riley takes the paper, but I can tell there's something else.

"What's wrong?" I ask.

"Well, a report just came in. A deputy tried to arrest Jed, and he attacked the deputy. He's okay. He just was knocked out cold, but Jed got away. They searched his house, and it's not good. Lots of drugs, some stolen guns."

Riley's legs give out. I catch her.

"I never saw him with drugs or guns at the house before I left," she says barely above a whisper.

Shane nods. "I've seen it before. You left, and he lost control and probably started the drugs to calm down, but they made him crazy and paranoid. There's also an open investigation with the deputy and department that didn't help you as well. There's a filed report, just like you said, so likely someone's losing their job."

She nods.

"What info does Jed have on her?" I ask.

"As I said, if he has anything, it's the town name, but there's an APB out on him. Attacking the officer was the worst thing he could do. We don't take lightly to that here. He's considered armed and dangerous. I'll put the word out in town. You know we protect our own."

I nod at Shane. "Please keep me updated."

"I will. It will be on the phone from now on, in case he happens to make it here. My guess is he'll be watching me to see if you show up again." I nod.

I carry Riley inside and sit on the couch. I call Colt and Sage. The ranch will be going into full-on lockdown, using the plans we put in place in case Sage's sperm donor got out and tried to come after her. Then I call Megan.

"Megan, listen. I know that you know what's going on with Riley I need a favor."

"Anything, big brother."

I explain what Shane told us.

"Can you stay with Hunter until this guy is caught?"

"What? Why?"

"Well one, if he shows up, I don't want him trailing you, and you leading him here. And two, if he shows up here, it will be safer if you aren't here."

She sighs and says she'll call Hunter and let me know.

She texts back letting me know Hunter said yes. She'll pack a bag tonight and head home with him.

I know Hunter will keep her safe. He's her best friend, but I know it's more than that. They've been dancing around it for a while.

"Riley baby, do you have a picture of Jed, so we know who to watch out for?"

She takes my phone and pulls up his Facebook profile. I save a few photos and send them to everyone.

I can tell he used to be a football player. He has the build and that arrogant smile. The kind that makes me want to toss my phone across the room.

"Blaze?"

"Yeah, baby."

"I don't want to be useless. Will you teach me to shoot a gun, please?"

Damn, this girl. She reminds me so much of Sage, and I'm so damn proud of her.

"Sure, let me grab a few things. There's a spot we use for practice not too far from the house. But can you make me a promise?"

"Maybe," she says.

I smile. "Promise me not to go anywhere alone not in the house, not around the ranch, and don't leave the property alone. Just for now."

"I can promise, but Blaze?"

"Yeah?"

"Can I sleep in your room? I'd feel... Safer." She looks down at her feet.

"I would sleep better with you with me too," I say. "Of course, you can."

Chapter 14

Riley

It has been a week since Jed escaped arrest. A week of sleeping in bed with Blaze, and I have to say, I feel so safe with him. I love his room too; it's very rustic.

He has a reclaimed wood wall where his bed is centered. His headboard is black leather, his nightstands are black, and his sheets are white and gray. He has a plush tan carpet. The room is so him, but it's comfortable enough that I love being there. And he loves having me there; he tells me so every night.

Blaze has taught me to shoot a gun, and I've gotten good. I also keep my promise to not go anywhere alone.

A few days ago, Brice came out and asked Sage to dinner. They've been on two dates, and Colt has stopped drinking and going out cold turkey. He's taking me with him to check on some horses, and I hope to pick his brain today.

"Can I ask you a question?" I ask Colt as we ride our horses along the fence line.

"What's up?" he asks.

"You ever going to forgive Sage?"

He looks like I just slapped him.

"She told me what happened a little bit and why she ran. I can tell her dating Brice is bothering you, so I'm just wondering."

He is quiet for so long I think he won't answer me.

"I hadn't realized until she started dating Brice that I hadn't forgiven her. I realized then how she felt about my behavior."

"She told me she came home for Megan's graduation and because of your... and I quote... man whoring, she left again. She couldn't watch it."

He sighs. "It's easy to get a reputation even if you don't earn it."

I look at him then. "What do you mean?"

"I wanted to hurt Sage like she hurt me. I was young and stupid, I get it. I let her think things. Hell, she still thinks them now. She'll never believe the truth."

"What's the truth?"

He shakes his head. "It doesn't matter."

"Colt, it does, and I think I'm breaking some friend code here, but she's only dating Brice because she doesn't want to go to the sale alone. She's tired of constantly being hurt and alone, but she still loves you."

His head snaps to me, and his horse stops. "She tell you that?"

I press my lips together. "I confronted her, and we talked. I see how you two look at each other. If you still love her, you're going to have to fight for her. You have both hurt each other, and it will take time, but if you really want it, stop letting everything hold you back. Life is short, and you aren't promised tomorrow. Don't you think you two have wasted enough time?"

We walk again, and I can tell Colt is lost in thought, so I keep quiet.

We finish our ride in silence, and I think I've done enough to help my friend.

When we get back to the barn, Blaze is there smiling at me. He helps me down from the horse.

"How was your ride?"

"Great, lots to think about," I say as I see Colt walk past.

"Take a walk with me?" Blaze asks.

He takes my hand, and we head down the driveway that goes behind the main house.

"I don't think I formally asked you, but will you be my date to the sale next weekend?" Blaze asks.

I smile. "Of course."

We walk a bit more, talking about the sale and entertainment after, how the sheriff will be there, and how he doesn't like how vulnerable it makes me with Jed still loose. He swears he won't leave my side for a moment, and I can tell he's stressed. I assure him I'll do as he asks, and he relaxes a bit.

Later that night, I'm up in Sage's room. We're trying to decide what to wear to the sale. I guess a dress is in order because of the dance after.

I decide on a simple form-fitting black dress and pair it with my jean jacket, brown belt, and boots. Simple but fun, and Sage approves.

We're sitting on her bed with some wine when I decide to come clean.

"I might have done something you'll be mad about," I say, chewing on my bottom lip.

"Oh Riley, I doubt it, but let's hear it."

"I talked to Colt on the ride today about you."

I watch her eyes flash with something I can't read before she covers it.

"About what?"

"I asked if he was ever going to forgive you."

"Oh, Riley." She sighs.

"That boy is still in love with you. He said he didn't realize how you felt until he saw you with Brice. He didn't know how much he hurt you until then."

Sage looks out the window but doesn't say anything.

"Then he said something that confused me. He said when you came back for Megan's graduation, he wanted to hurt you, and he let you believe something that wasn't true. He doesn't think you'll believe the truth now. He didn't explain, but maybe you know what he means."

I see Sage wipe her eyes. "Well, only time will tell, huh?"

I nod. Just then, a siren sounds and Sage lunges for her gun and grabs my arm at the same time.

"That's the house alarm. Fuck!" She pulls me into her closet and opens a secret door behind some clothes.

"Stay here. Don't make a sound until Blaze or I come for you. Got it?"

I nod. Just as she closes the door, everything goes black.

Chapter 15

Blaze

The second the house alarm goes off, everyone drops everything and runs faster than I've ever seen toward the house. Colt is beside me as we reach the house, and I look at him. "Sage and Riley were in her room last I knew."

He nods and heads to the back door as the ranch hands circle the house. I head to the front door and quietly make my way inside. There's nothing out of place. Colt coming through the back shakes his head, indicating he's seen nothing. I do the same. He heads to the wing with Sage's office, and I check the wing with the mother-in-law suite, meant for a housekeeper if we had one.

Colt and I come out. The ranch hands are at both doors, so we head upstairs. Sage is by her bedroom. She shakes her head just as the alarm silences. Mac or Jason must have got here. I move toward Sage, clearing room after room, and Colt clears the guest wing.

Nothing. Colt runs down the hall and before I know it, he has Sage in his arms.

"What happened?" Colt asks.

"We were sitting on the bed just talking, and it went off. She's in the closet." We both nod and wait for Mac and Jason to join us.

Jason rounds the stairs first, gun in hand. Mac follows.

"It doesn't make sense." Jason shakes his head. "It was tripped at the living room window, but there's nothing. No footprints, no sign of entry, nothing out of place. The windows are locked. We covered the floor again and nothing."

I head to Sage's closet. The five of us are the only ones who know about the hidden room. It's Sage's safe room if ever needed. I've never been so glad to have it.

"Riley baby, it's Blaze," I say as I open the door. She jumps into my arms, almost knocking me over. I carry her out to the couch and see Sage in Colt's arms, her head on his chest. His face looks like he's holding his whole world.

"Blaze, what happened?" Riley pulls my attention away.

"A false alarm, baby. We cleared the house. There's nothing. We checked what triggered the alarm, and there's nothing." I feel her shaking, and it's my undoing.

I pick her up and carry her past Sage and Colt. "You got her?" I ask, referring to Sage.

"We're good," he says and nods, leading Sage to her room.

I take Riley to my room, kick the door closed behind me, and lay her on the bed. I take my shoes off and place my gun on my nightstand, lie down next to her, and pull her close.

We just lie in each other's arms for a bit before I lift my head to hers and kiss her. The kiss soothes my soul and kicks my heart into overdrive at the same time.

We stay in bed until dinner time, and I never let her out of my arms. At dinner that night, I never stop holding her hand. I can't. I need to reassure myself that she's here and okay.

• • • • • • • • • •

Riley

It's the day of the cattle sale, and Sage, Megan, and I are getting ready together.

There hasn't been a peep from Jed. Authorities are still looking for him, and I can tell everyone has been tense here.

Heck, Sage has picked out her dress based on what hides her gun best. They aren't joking or taking chances, and I love them for that.

It makes me feel loved but at the same time, I feel guilty that they're going through all this for me.

I can't keep putting Blaze or even myself through this. It's too much, but I don't have it in me to leave like I should. I finally feel like I belong for the first time since my parents died. I might be selfish, but I'm not willing to give that up.

I'm still shaken about the alarm, and Blaze has asked me to stay back at the house tonight with Mac and Jason, but I know they both want to be at the sale. I don't want to be a burden. Besides, I can't hide forever, right?

Once dressed, we head downstairs where Hunter, who is Megan's date, and Blaze are waiting.

Watching his eyes go wide when he sees me is exciting.

"Riley, you're so beautiful. I don't have words," Blaze says, and I know I blush.

The doorbell rings and while we all tense, Sage walks over and answers to find Brice, her date. Then we all head over to the other side of the ranch together.

I love sitting in the bleachers, watching the sale. I can't understand the auctioneer to save my life, but the buzz around everyone is contagious.

After the sale, we head to a big entertaining barn that's done up with tables, a buffet, a bar, a dance floor, and twinkle lights everywhere.

I'm having a great time, but I can't help but scan the crowd for signs of Jed more often than I'd like. I can tell Blaze does the same thing.

Blaze is talking to an older gentleman, and I watch Colt walk the perimeter of the barn, taking everything in. I see the moment his eyes land on Sage who is dancing with Brice.

I hope those two can work out their issues. They're so in love with each other.

Blaze squeezes my hand to get my attention. "May I have this dance?" he asks as if I would say no.

I smile, and he leads me to the dance floor.

"Are you having a good time?" Blaze asks.

"I am. I love the community in this town. I'm glad this is where I ended up that night."

Blaze pulls me in closer. "Me too."

When one song ends, and another begins, Blaze runs his hand up my back.

"Next month, there's a big gala in Dallas. It's for the ranchers and since we're the second biggest ranch in the state, we're expected to go. I'd love for you to be my date. I'll cover the dress; it has to be a Texas formal. Sage can help you go shopping."

I smile. "I'd love to go with you."

"I was thinking of getting a room at the hotel for that night, instead of driving back. It doesn't get out until late. We all normally do."

"That sounds good, but who do you mean by 'we all?'"

"Well, Mom and Dad go and since we run this ranch equally, so does Colt, Sage, Mac, Jason, Megan, and me. Megan normally brings Hunter, and Sage normally goes with me, but I guess she would go with Brice this year. Colt, Mac, and Jason go stag."

I nod, and we keep dancing. As the song ends, I get this feeling of being watched, making the hair on the back of my neck stand.

My eyes dart around the building, and I don't see anything out of place. I try to focus on the shadows where it's hard to see.

"What's wrong?" Blaze asks. He must have felt me tense up.

"Nothing," I say and smile at him, not wanting to upset him over nothing.

I feel like I'm just missing something out of the corner of my eye, so I keep watching. Then I see him. I swear it looks like Jed walking out of the back door.

"He's here," I barely whisper. Blaze whips around.

"Where?" he says, placing his hands on my arms.

I point to the doors as I watch his back walking through them. Blaze gets Colt's attention, and they go after him. I want to run back to the house and hide in bed, but my feet carry me toward Jed.

We get outside but when the man turns around it's not Jed. I gasp in a breath of relief, and panic washes over me. Is it always going to be like this?

I feel Blaze's arms around me.

"Come on, baby, let me get you home."

Before I know it, I'm back at the house and all I can think about is that there's still no sign of Jed. I should be happy about that, but I can't help but wonder if I'll always see him in the crowd.

As I get ready for bed, I think things over. Life here is balancing on a thin line. A small tip will have it all crashing down.

Chapter 16

Blaze

I've been running around all day today with meetings before the Cattleman's Association Gala tonight. Riley has been with Sage and Megan in Sage's room, getting ready, and my mind has been on Riley.

It has been a month since the sale at the ranch, and Riley and I have been dating. I've taken her out to dinner a few times but mostly, we do a lot of dates on the ranch.

She loves riding the horses or sneaking away to one of the cabins, cooking dinner, and spending time with just us. I love that time too because I don't have to share her attention.

Things have been perfect, well, except she won't sleep in my bed anymore. I feel like there's still a wall up with her. I've been able to break down several, she's opened up about Jed and her aunt. She has told me about her parents, but she's still holding herself back.

I can't say I blame the girl after what she has been through. I'm more than willing to earn it and take my time. The last thing I want to do is rush her.

We all arrive in Dallas and get an early check-in at the hotel. I'm hoping I can convince Riley to come back to my room tonight, so I can fall asleep with her in my arms. I miss that most of all. If the guys could only hear me now, I'm sure they would make me hand in my man card.

I get to my room and rush through a shower and get dressed. Since this is cowboy formal, I'm in a pair of dark dress jeans with a white button-down shirt, a black sports coat, my cowboy boots, and my black dress hat. This is how we do formal here.

I check the time, and I have twenty minutes to spare, so I sit and check my phone. I've been watching for any sign of Jed and even hired a private investigator to help track him down. So far, nothing.

I want to give Riley the peace of mind that he can't hurt her anymore. I feel like that's the last thing holding her back, the fact that he can resurface at any time.

We've told her more times than I can count. This is her home now, and she isn't going anywhere. I know in the back of her head, there's a small doubt since everyone had always sent her back to him. Time will show her... we mean what we say.

Heading down the hall to Sage's room, I knock on the door. I can't help but smile when I hear Sage telling Riley to get the door because it's her man. Damn right, I'm her man. But I'm not prepared for the sight in front of me when Riley opens the door.

She's in an off-white lacy dress with a high hemline that shows off her cowboy boots. She has a thick brown belt on and some amazing turquoise jewelry I know is from the reservation. Her hair is down with some mouthwatering curls. I just want to wrap them around my fist and pull her to me...

Whoa boy, deep breath before I end up taking her against the wall in the hallway.

"Riley, you take my breath away." She has short-circuited my brain, and I can't think of anything else.

"Thank you." She gives me one of her blinding smiles.

I offer her my arm, and we head down to the ballroom. People are already milling around and talking. There's a bar and appetizers are being walked around.

I guide her to the bar to get her a drink even though she only wants a soda. I stick to just a soda as well, knowing her experience with alcohol and Jed. We see Mom and Dad who come up to hug Riley and talk for a minute before George King walks up.

"Well, hello there, Blaze. Who do we have here?" George says, pulling off what anyone who didn't know him would assume is friendly.

"George, this is my girlfriend Riley. Riley this is George King. He owns the largest ranch in Texas."

He takes Riley's hand and kisses it. It takes everything in me not to yank her hand away from him.

"Well, I'm not sure what such a beautiful young lady is doing with only the second largest ranch in the state, but if you tire of him, you're welcome down at a real ranch any time," George says.

Thankfully, Dad steps in. "Well, size doesn't matter much if the profit isn't there." Dad jabs at him since last year when we made more money than they did. It was only by a hundred dollars, but it's been a running competition from day one.

Though we have Sage and her horse training to thank for the win there.

I can tell George doesn't like that thrown in his face. Riley can too.

"What? You can dish it but not take it, George?" Riley says in her sweet-as-sin voice. No one says a word as George's eyes snap to hers.

Then he laughs, a full belly laugh that draws attention from around the room. "Beautiful and sharp witted. I like her. Hold on to her, Blaze. She won't stay on the market long if you don't."

He shakes our hands and moves on to his next round of conversation.

"I'm sorry. I shouldn't have said that. I think Sage is rubbing off on me. I didn't think before I spoke," Riley says.

Dad laughs. "Don't you worry about it. You just became part of the family, is all. Everyone here gives George a good ribbing time and again." Dad pats her shoulder as he and Mom are pulled away.

I still see a bit of worry in her eyes.

"I promise it was fine. My comeback was much worse, so you did me a favor." I smile at her.

"Do you know all these people?" she asks.

"No, but a lot of them. Sage comes because she drums up business for her horse training. Dad and Colt will make contacts to breed some of our horses and bulls this year. Normally, I help with that but this year, I'm showing you the ropes."

"So, this is a big networking event?"

"Basically, a lot of deals are made here. Relationships are built too."

"What can I do to help?" she asks, and I smile.

"Honestly, get to know people. Talk to the wives and get your face known. Next year, you'll be helping Sage make contacts for the horses, but this year, just get to know people."

She nods, and we make the rounds. I introduce her to people, and we hold many conversations before it's time to sit at our table for dinner.

"We aren't sitting with your family?" Riley asks.

"No, dinner is another networking opportunity. We like to spread out."

She nods. "It's easier when you have such a big family," she says as I pull out her chair.

"It is. Mac, Jason, and Megan come to network for the ranch too. Mac talks a lot with other foremen and networks for hiring people. Jason and Megan do a lot of events. They've even rented out our event barn to several functions just from this gala alone. Hunter helps them out too, but I suspect he's gained a few patients as well."

We chat with the other couples at our table over our steak dinner. This year, the steak is from the Deep River Ranch. They make a decent presentation on their ranch and how they raise their cattle.

"Why isn't your ranch or King's ranch the one supplying the steak since you're bigger?" Riley leans over and asks.

"It's a lottery system. If you can supply the food and meet the association requirements, you put your name in the lottery. We did it three years ago. King did it last year. Our turn will come up again," I tell her, but my heart warms that she cares so much about everything going on tonight.

I watch Riley talking to the couple next to her, and I can tell they're under her spell just like I am. It's so easy to see why I love this girl.

Woah.

Love. Yes, holy shit, I'm in love with Riley. I guess I've known it for a while. When I picture my future, it's been with her. She has been mine from the moment I first saw her, but I never admitted it. Now, when do I tell her? I don't want to scare her off, but I want her to know I'm all in too.

When dinner ends, the music starts back up.

"Would you like to dance?" I ask Riley, and she beams up at me.

"I'd love to."

I lead her out to the dance floor and take her hand in mine. I place my other hand on her waist and pull her close. She rests her hand on my shoulder, and we start a gentle sway to the music. I watch Dad lead Mom out to the dance floor too.

"Aww." Riley looks over my shoulder.

"What is it?" I ask.

"Colt and Sage are dancing together." I smile.

"I don't know what is up between those two, but I hope they figure it out. Oh, look. Hunter is pulling Megan onto the dance floor."

"Think Mac and Jason will find someone to dance with?"

I laugh "The wives always pull them to the floor for a dance with a handsome young fellow as they say, so their dance cards will be filled. Don't you worry."

We dance through three more songs, just talking about the night and taking each other in. Having her so close, her rubbing up against me has my body on a live wire. My cock is so hard behind my zipper, I could hammer nails. All I can think about is getting her alone.

After the next song ends, I lean down to Riley's ear.

"You ready to get out of here? I was hoping you'd come back to my room with me."

She hesitates. "I don't know, Blaze."

"I just want to hold you in my arms tonight. Nothing will happen that you don't want, I promise. I just need to hold you."

She looks up at me and then nods.

Chapter 17

Blaze

We sneak our way out, saying good night to the guys and Megan, but we can't seem to find Sage. I place my hand on Riley's lower back and guide her toward the elevators.

"I just need to stop at Sage's room and get my stuff," she says.

Soon as we're in the elevator, I have her pinned against the wall with my lips on hers. It's a hard and passion-filled kiss but since the ride to our floor is short, so is the kiss. When the doors open, I pull away.

"I've been wanting to do that all night," I say, and she smiles.

"Me too."

Damn, I think several cold showers are in my future tonight. We stop outside Sage's room, where Riley grabs her bag and leaves her key for Sage along with a note telling her where she is.

"All set?" I ask as I take her bag from her.

"I am," she says, and I take her hand as we head down the hallway to my room. I open the door and follow her in.

I set her bag on the dresser and look at her. She's so beautiful, I can't seem to keep my hands off her.

Before I know it, I'm in front of her, and my lips are on her again. I keep the kiss soft and sweet. Her hands lift into my hair at the back of my neck, and she pulls me closer. I know she can feel how hard I am for her.

I run my hands down her sides to her hips and around her back to her perfect ass and pull her against me. I feel her grind against my cock, and I lose it. I guide her to the bed and lay her down.

I pull back and look at her. She looks like an angel across the white sheet, her hair splayed out around her. The slight blush on her cheeks, it all has my cock dripping cum.

"Blaze," she whispers. In an instant, I'm lying on the bed right beside her, and my lips are back on hers, with my hand on her hip.

"I want you," she whispers against my mouth.

"You have me, baby," I murmur back and kiss down her neck and below her ear.

"I want you inside me, Blaze," she says, and my breath catches.

I pull back to look into her eyes. There's no fear or hesitation. "Are you sure, baby? Once I'm inside you, you're mine for good. I won't be able to let you go or let you walk away."

"That's what I want. Make me yours, Blaze," she says and sits up. She removes her dress, leaving her only in a thin, lacy bra and her barely-there lace thong.

Cum leaks from my cock, and I can't stop the groan that leaves me as I stand and reach for her.

"God, you're the most beautiful thing I've ever seen," I say.

"And you have way too many clothes on."

I remove my jacket, and she slowly, tortuously, unbuttons my shirt, pushing her hands against my bare chest to move the shirt off my shoulders. It floats to the floor.

She leans forward and places a kiss in the center of my chest, causing my whole body to shiver at her touch. Her hands trail down to the waist of my pants and slowly unbutton them, pulling the zipper down.

My pants hit the floor, and my mouth lands on hers as I guide her back to the bed. I kiss down her neck and between the swell of her breasts before reaching around to remove her bra.

Her perfect breasts tumble out, and I take one in each hand and give them a good squeeze, watching her face to see her reaction. I lower my head and take one nipple in my mouth while I pinch the other between my fingers.

Riley moans, and her back arches toward me. I release her nipple and move to the other side, giving all parts of my girl equal attention. Then I kiss my way down her stomach to the top of her panties.

I run my finger over her slit, above the thin fabric.

"Baby, you're soaked," I moan.

"See what you do to me?" she says, and it causes me to lose the last of my control.

I rip her panties from her and toss them to the ground. I pull her thighs apart and take a long, light swipe of her from her slit to her clit.

"Blaze," she yells and grabs my hair.

I continue to circle my tongue around her hard nub, feeling her pussy pulse. I know she's close. I thrust a finger inside her, and her hips arch. Feeling her wet, warm pulse around me is almost my undoing.

I add a second finger and curl them up to find her G-spot. With just a few strokes, her body locks up, and she's screaming my name while her juices fill my mouth and run down her thighs. I love every minute of it, and I have a brief thought that I hope our neighbors aren't any of our family. She's screaming so loud, there's no way to hide it.

When she relaxes, I kiss my way back up her stomach, between her breasts, giving each nipple a firm suck, causing her body to shudder each time.

Then I kiss her mouth, hard and firm, and pull my boxers down and reach for my wallet to grab a condom and slip it on. I brace myself over her at her warm, wet entrance.

"Last chance, baby. You sure about this?" I ask, knowing I'll be crushed and have a severe case of blue balls if she's changed her mind.

"Mmmm," she hums and then looks at me with glassy, passion-filled eyes. "I'm yours, Blaze. I want this," she says as she wraps her arms around my neck and her legs around my hips.

"Look at me, baby. Watch me as I make you mine," I say. When her eyes meet mine, I slide inside of her so slowly, feeling her stretch. I rock my hips until I'm fully seated inside her, and her pussy is contracting around me.

I have to pause for a minute before I embarrass myself. She's so hot and wet and perfect, I could come right now. She squirms under me, and it's almost too much to take.

"Baby, I need a minute," I groan, and she settles. In the next breath, she's arching her back again.

"Blaze, oh God, I need you to move or I might explode." I smile into her neck and start slow, even thrusts.

I reach down and pull her hips even closer to me as I sit up on my knees still thrusting into her. At this angle, I can tell I'm hitting her G-spot with each thrust. She bucks her hips, moaning my name.

Another thrust and I feel her orgasm crash into her. I think about all the things I need to order at the ranch and spreadsheets to keep from coming right along with her.

When she relaxes, I lean over and wrap my arms around her back, pulling her up so she sits on my lap. With my knees still bent, she wraps her arms around my neck and her legs around my waist.

I support her back and thrust into her again, telling her how good she feels and how tight she is.

I feel her getting close again and adjust my angle, so every thrust has my pubic bone hitting her clit. After a few more thrusts, she climaxes again. This time, I follow her over the edge. Her pussy squeezes my cock so hard, it causes me to blackout.

I lay her down on the bed and roll to the side to not crush her while we catch our breaths.

"Wow," she gasps. "I never knew sex could be like that."

The caveman in me wants to come out and pound on my chest, but I only have the energy to smile.

"It's because it's us. Our connection means everything," I say and roll to my side and prop my head up on my hand to look down at her.

When her eyes meet mine, I reach down and smooth some hair away from her face and lightly brush my lips against hers. Then I sit up and wait for her eyes to meet mine again.

"I love you, Riley. That was the best sex I've ever had. It's because it's us."

Her eyes get watery, and she reaches up to rest her hand against my face.

"I love you too, Blaze, so much."

I smile at her "You're mine now, Riley; no backing out, no turning back."

She smiles and shakes her head. "I'm not going anywhere."

I lean down and kiss her again before I get up to dispose of the condom. I come back to the bed with a warm, wet washcloth.

"Spread your legs, baby. Let me clean you up," I say.

She spreads her legs and watches me with a lazy smile on her face. I toss the washcloth back into the bathroom and lie in bed and pull her against me.

I listen to her breathing until I hear steady even breaths that let me know she's fallen asleep.

I soak in the warmth of her skin on mine, thinking about my life with Riley. I can't wait to start on our forever. I'd ask her to marry me tomorrow if I knew she would say yes.

The only thing standing in our way is Jed. I don't want her constantly living in fear of him, clouding any happiness Riley might gain. I need to redouble my efforts to find him when we get home tomorrow.

I make myself and Riley a promise to do anything it takes to find Jed sooner rather than later.

Chapter 18

Riley

It's been a few days since the Cattleman's Gala, and I've been in Blaze's bed every night as we explore each other's bodies, learning what the other likes. I wake up each morning with Blaze's head between my legs.

Let me tell you, waking up to an orgasm is the best thing ever. There's nothing that can beat it. It's even better than the best cup of coffee.

This morning, I wake up, and Blaze is still asleep, but our phones are going off like crazy. I reach for mine and see it's a group text with Sage, Megan, the guys, and their parents.

I look at the first text in the string, and it's a link from Helen. I click it and open it to find an article on the Cattleman's Gala. Innocent enough until I scroll down and see a picture of Blaze talking to George King with his arms wrapped around me.

The caption lists both ranch names as well as George and Blaze's names.

Texts keep coming in.

Colt: Holy fuck, this is normally good news but not if it's public.

Mac: Are they even up yet? Have they seen this?

Sage: No, I think they're still asleep. Their door is closed.

Helen: Well, I bet all these texts wake them up.

Jason: We need to lock down the property ASAP.

Colt: We have been on lockdown.

Panic rips through me. I know what they're talking about. Jed can easily see this and know exactly where I am. I reach over and nudge Blaze to wake him up.

"More cuddles," he says in his gravelly morning voice, which normally has me wet and ready to go instantly.

"Blaze, wake up. It's bad," I say as my phone keeps going off.

That causes him to sit right up. "What's wrong?"

I hand him my phone with the article pulled up and show it to him.

"Fuck," he mutters. In an instant, we're up and getting dressed.

Another text comes in.

Blaze: Meeting. Kitchen. Now.

We all get downstairs and get some coffee Tim and Helen walk in, and Megan texts, saying to fill her in when we're done because she's already in town.

Everyone talks plans on tightening up the security, Mac suggests asking some of his friends from the reservation to come over and help keep an eye on the place. They agree, and Mac heads out.

Sage turns to me, and I can feel her trying to get a read on me before she speaks. That's what Sage does.

"Listen, I have some work to do here in my office. I want to do some freezer meals and get stocked up for Hell Week coming up. We'll be working from sun up to sundown, getting ready for winter. Why don't you stay with me? We'll set the alarm, listen to some music, and just take a down day while the guys get the ranch in order."

I see her looking over my shoulder, and I know she's looking at Blaze. "I'm sure it will give the guys peace of mind to know you're in the house with the alarm on."

I know she's right. Plus, I don't want to admit the idea of walking around the ranch, looking over my shoulder every few minutes, doesn't appeal to me.

I won't admit I'm a bit more than worried. That article was posted yesterday afternoon, and we're all just seeing it this morning. Jed could be on the property already waiting and watching. I think everyone is thinking the same thing, but no one wants to say anything.

I force a smile. "That would be great, Sage."

The guys all head out, but Blaze lingers behind and pulls me into a tight hug.

"Stay by Sage today, please. Be her shadow. Maybe even consider having her in the bathroom when you pee, just for my peace of mind."

I smile at that. "I'll do everything she says and promise to stay in the house. Go out there and get everything done. Come back to me because all I want to do is crawl into bed with you and snuggle in for the day."

Blaze kisses my forehead, and I can feel the smile on his lips.

"That sounds like heaven, baby. Be safe, call or text me. Let me know you're okay and try to relax. We'll take care of you," he says before leaning down to give me a passionate kiss.

He takes control of my mouth and when I gasp, his tongue finds mine. We both get so lost in the kiss, we don't break apart until we hear someone cough. Even then, when Blaze pulls away, he rests his forehead on mine to catch his breath.

I look over and see Sage smiling. "I promise not to let her out of my sight, Blaze."

Blaze nods and kisses my forehead before heading out. Sage makes sure the door is locked and sets the alarm.

"Okay, bookwork first. You can read in my office with me if you want?" Sage asks.

"That sounds perfect."

Sage works, and I read for a few hours until lunchtime. Since all the guys are heading to Tom and Helen's side of the ranch for lunch today, it's just Sage and me. As we make our way into the kitchen, I send Blaze a quick text.

Me: Leftover mac and cheese for lunch here. What are you having?

Blaze: Meatloaf sandwiches.

Me: Ugh, you win!

Blaze: LOL! You girls doing okay?

Me: Yeah, Sage finished her office work. We're going to start cooking after lunch.

Going to crank on some music and make it an afternoon.

Blaze: Sounds good, baby. Stay safe, send me some photos of the food you make.

Me: Will do. Love you.

Blaze: Love you too.

After lunch, Sage and I start cooking some chicken, peeling potatoes, and browning ground beef. Sage also has a huge pot of homemade sauce cooking on the stove too.

We're having a great afternoon talking and listening to music that we forget about Jed and the reason we're housebound today. I'm reaching for the sweet tea in the fridge to refill our glasses when I hear glass shattering. Thinking Sage dropped something, I get ready to ask her if she's okay. Before the word leaves my mouth, the house alarm goes off.

Sage's eyes meet mine, and I watch her face pale. She reaches for her gun on the counter and rushes out to the living room where the sound of glass came from. I send up a silent prayer that the guys come running like they did last time and follow Sage into the main part of the house.

What I see freezes me in my tracks. Jed is standing inside the living room between Sage and myself. It looks like he got in and

THE COWBOY AND HIS RUNAWAY

somehow came up behind Sage when she walked in, but it doesn't look like the Jed I know. His clothes are dirty and stained, and he looks like he hasn't showered in days. I've seen homeless people look in better shape than he does.

I must have made a noise because it's enough that he gets a jump on Sage and knocks her gun across the room and pulls a knife on her. He has his arm around her shoulder and the knife at her throat.

"Look at you, you high-class slut. Traded me in for your new boyfriend so easily, didn't you?"

Sage looks so calm and is staying quiet, but I know she's biding her time, making sure the guys are close and waiting for the right moment.

"Jed, let Sage go. This isn't about her."

"Oh, it is. They took you in and kept you from me. This is just as much about them as it is about you. Where's your new *boyfriend*?" he spits out.

"I don't know. He had to check on the cattle today," I say, keeping things as close to the truth as possible.

"Well, since I'm sure the whole ranch can hear this alarm, it shouldn't be long before he gets here," he says and inches closer to me. "How about we have a little fun until then. I'm going to have him watch as I show him you're mine."

He lunges at me, and the next thing I feel is lightning-hot heat on the side of my face. My vision goes dark, and I feel myself hit the wall then the floor. The metallic taste of blood fills my mouth. My vision comes back, but everything is blurry until I hear a gunshot, and everything goes black again.

Chapter 19

Blaze

I'm at the back of the barn, talking to the guys from the reservation when the house alarm goes off.

"Fuck!" I roar, and we all run toward the house, pulling out our guns at the same time. Jason, Mac, and Colt meet me at the front of the barn. I nod and without a word, we execute the plan we put in place this morning with no hesitation.

Jason and Mac run around the back of the house with the guys Mac brought back from the reservation. Colt goes to the kitchen door with a few ranch hands, and I head to the front door with a few more ranch hands.

The others surround the house outside and wait for instructions.

I get to the front of the house, and I see the broken glass at the front window and motion to the guys behind me to be silent. They nod in response, and I head toward the window. I don't need to look in to know what's going on.

The voice I hear floating out the window has my blood boiling.

"Look at you, you high-class slut. Trade me in for your new boyfriend so easily, didn't you?"

I turn back to the guys and walk away from the window. I turn to one and say, "Run back to the office in the barn. Call the sheriff and tell him I told you to call and that Jed broke into the house. Ask him to hurry. Then call my parents and tell them what's going on. Tell them to call Megan to make sure she stays in town. Then get back out here." He nods and runs off.

I take a deep breath and head to the front door. I know it's locked, so I pull out my keys, praying I can unlock the door quietly. The sound of the alarm should drown out any sound of the lock turning.

Just as I open the door, I hear a loud thud. When I get the door open, the sight breaks my heart. Riley is on the floor against the wall, and her lip is split wide open. Sage is wrestling with Jed, trying to get a large knife out of his hand.

He lunges the knife at Sage and manages to slice her chest. Blood rolls and stains her shirt bright red.

Where the hell is Sage's gun?

Jed sees me, and his wild eyes focus on me. Sage tries to take him down again, but he backhands her, making me cringe. She goes flying to the floor. A second later, there's a sickening thud as her head hits the floor.

I see Jason and Mac coming up behind him. He makes a move toward me and with both girls clear, I don't even blink an eye as I raise my gun and pull the trigger. His body slumps to the ground. I don't even check on him. I run right to Riley and pull her in my arms.

"Riley, baby, are you okay?"

It takes a painful, heart stopping moment for her to open her eyes.

"I think so. What happened?"

I look up to see Mac leaning over Jed, shaking his head.

"I'm fine," I say.

"The gunshot?" she asks.

"Went right between Jed's eyes. You won't ever have to deal with him again."

She starts to turn her head but I pull her into my chest. "No, baby, don't look. You don't need to see that."

I see Jason come over to Sage after turning off the alarm. Colt is over by Sage, who's still out; my heart stills.

"Sage, love, wake up. Don't do this to me again. Please wake up," Colt pleads as he pushes some hair from Sage's face. Her eyes are still closed, but she starts to stir.

Colt sits up and pulls his shirt off, pressing it on her chest where the knife cut her.

Sage finally opens her eyes and looks at him. "Colt?"

"Oh, thank God, love. Are you okay?" Colt leans down, lightly pressing his forehead to hers.

"Jed cut you pretty good, and you hit your head when you fell. We need to get you checked out." Just as he says this, we can hear the faint sound of sirens.

"I got the gate," Mac says and runs off.

"I'll call Mom and Dad and Megan. We'll get the ranch hands settled and meet you at the hospital." Jason says and tilts his chin toward where Mac has run off.

I nod and look back down at Riley. She has been taking it all in like I had. Her eyes meet mine, and relief washes over me.

The sheriff walks in, looks at us, and shakes his head. I keep Riley's head against my chest. The sight in front of us isn't pretty, something she never needs to see.

Sage gets loaded in the ambulance, and Colt rides with her. I insist that Riley be seen as well, and we follow behind them in my truck. Mom and Dad stay behind with the sheriff. He says he'll meet us at the hospital for questioning.

We sit in the emergency room for an hour before we're released. Riley gets the all clear. She just has a split lip which will heal on its own. She'll likely have a killer headache for the next day or so. The doctor says to keep an eye on her for signs of a possible concussion, but she looks good to go.

Colt has been texting updates the whole time. When Jason and Mac get to the hospital, I send them to Sage's room because we're almost done. Now Riley has the all clear, we head to see Sage.

A nurse stops us outside her room.

"I'm sorry, sir. Family only," she says at the same time she's basically eye-fucking me. It really pisses me off since I'm holding Riley's hand in mine.

"This is my sister's room," I say. She nods, looks at Riley, and opens her mouth to say something. "And this is my wife." I cut her off and pull Riley with me into the room.

"Hey, any updates?" I ask Colt when we walk in.

"They're keeping her overnight. She's showing signs of a mild concussion. She had to have stitches on the cut, so they want to monitor that for infection. She lost a good amount of blood, and she's right on the edge of needing a transfusion. They're watching that as well." He's holding Sage's hand and looking at her the way I had looked at Riley in her hospital bed downstairs. I need to ask him about that later.

Over the next hour, Jason, Mac, Megan, Hunter, Mom, and Dad all trickle in. The sheriff and a few deputies come in to take a report on both Riley and Sage's injuries then pull us all aside in a conference room down the hall for questioning. They make us all leave the room when it's Sage's turn. Colt refuses, and the sheriff allows him to stay, knowing both of their pasts.

When we're all done, Sage falls asleep. I see Colt fighting sleep as well. I know he won't leave her side; never did the last time she was in the hospital either.

"Hey, we're going to head home. Riley needs to rest too. You got her?" I ask Colt and point to Sage. He nods while looking at her.

"Yeah, I'm not going anywhere."

"You need anything?" I ask.

"Just for her to be okay."

"I think she will be. Text or call if you need anything."

Everyone heads home.

When I pull up to the house, Mom follows us in. I'm about to protest when she puts her hand up.

"Listen, it's been a long day. You both need to eat, and the living room needs to be cleaned, not to mention the window can't be fixed until tomorrow. Why don't you pack a bag for you and her and head to our house? Megan went over to heat the lasagna and once the food is done, she's going to come over. We'll clean up here, so you guys don't have to worry about it."

I can't do anything but nod. I reach in and hug Mom and try not to let the tears fall from my eyes. My parents are the most amazing people I know. They know just what we need, and they're always there. Heck, they took in three teens who needed a home and never blinked an eye. They gave me this amazing family, and I could never express how much I love them.

"Thank you, Mom," I say and kiss her on the cheek. I sit Riley down at the dining room table and run upstairs.

I grab one of my old duffel bags and toss in two days' worth of clothes and my bathroom items and then head to Riley's room where she still keeps her clothes and toss in clothes and her bathroom items and then run back downstairs.

I drive Riley over to Mom and Dad's, and we head right up to my old room. We both head right to bed and cuddle up. Riley falls asleep almost instantly, but I can't seem to get my mind to shut off.

I hear a light knock on the door and see Megan standing there. She smiles. "Dinner is cooling off on the stove. There's lasagna and garlic bread."

"Thanks, Megs. I'll wake her up in a bit to head down and eat."

She nods. "Is it okay if I move back home now? I like living with Hunter and all, but I miss all you guys more."

I smile. "It hasn't been the same without you, so you better be home tonight." I try to smile.

Megan leans against the door, and I can tell something is on her mind.

"What is it, Megs?"

"Well, you know I'm a grown adult now, right? I know Sage, Colt, and Mac got dealt a shit hand with bio parents, and I have a general idea of what happened. I appreciate you guys protecting me back then, I really do. I just don't want you to do it anymore. This is my family too, and I want to protect it when necessary. Do things like this scare me? Yes, but I should have been there today with them. I don't know if it would have helped, but I should have been there..." she trails off.

I sigh. "I'm sorry, Megs. You're right. We did protect you from a lot growing up. It wasn't pretty, and neither was what happened today. For the record, I protected Riley too. I wouldn't let her look at Jed once I shot him. It's an image you don't need to see. Ask Sage, there are some things you should avoid at all costs."

"I understand, but don't force me from my own home again, okay?"

I smile. "I promise, Megs. I love you."

"Love you too, B."

Chapter 20

Riley

I wake up in Blaze's old bedroom and see the sun has set.

"Hey, beautiful. Dinner is waiting for us downstairs. I was going to wake you up in about ten more minutes."

I look over at Blaze, and his face is so serious.

"I was so scared today when I saw him there. I can't lose you, baby. I love you so damn much. It would destroy me."

I feel tears in my eyes. I bring my hand to the side of his face and feel him lean into my touch.

"The same goes for me too, baby. I'm so thankful to you for saving us, so relieved he's gone. I feel so safe now thanks to you, but my heart hurts for that burden you now have to carry because of me."

His lips are on mine in a hard but sweet kiss before pulling away.

"I would do anything for you, Riley. I've been thinking about this and while killing someone was never on my list of things to do in life, I didn't hesitate, and I wouldn't hesitate if I was put back in the situation again. I know what he did to you. I heard what he had planned, and he was a threat to not only your safety but Sage and the rest of my family too. I don't regret it, not one bit."

"I love you, Blaze."

"I love you too. Now let's eat."

· · · ● · ● · · ·

The next morning, I wake up and reach for Blaze, but I find a cold and empty bed. I stretch, and then I see a note on his pillow.

Riley,

You looked so peaceful sleeping I couldn't bring myself to wake you. I know after yesterday you need your sleep.

I'm heading over to the house to make sure everything is cleaned up and install a new window, so we can all go home tonight.

Mom and Megan will be downstairs when you wake up. They want to spend the day with you.

I'll see you at dinner.

I love you with everything I am.
Blaze

I can't help but smile at that. He's the most amazing man in the world. He has shown me over and over that he's nothing like Jed.

From the little things like small touches and kisses, to how he shows his dominance. He can make sure everyone knows I'm his, like at the gala, but in a way that makes me feel safe and loved.

He protects me, like yesterday with Jed, but I know if I had pushed the issue, he would have let me see him lying on the floor. I just had no reason to want to. I felt safe and loved in his arms.

He doesn't keep me hidden away. He loved showing me off at the sale and the gala. Because of him, I have these friends who consider me family.

I'm set to start school online next month, and any little thing I ask for, he does. I have to be careful though. I pointed out a shirt I liked, and it was in my closet the next day.

I smile and think about everything that has brought me here.

Lilly.

I grab my phone and find her number in my wallet. It's almost ten a.m. so I take a chance and call her.

"Hello?"

"Lilly?"

"Yes."

"This is Riley. I don't know if you'll remember me..."

"Riley, oh my word, I'm so happy to hear from you!! You've been on my mind every time I pass through Rock Springs!"

I laugh. "You were on my mind this morning, and I wanted to reach out and thank you for what you did taking a chance and stopping to pick me up that night."

"Oh honey, I'd do it again a million times over. Has there been any more problems from the guy?"

"Well, my friends convinced me to press charges. I did, and he ran. He showed up here just yesterday and after attacking me and my friend... well, he's dead. He won't bother me again."

"Oh, I'm glad. Sorry a life had to be lost but can't say he'll be missed. I'm glad your friend came through to help you."

"Well, a little confession. When I got out of your truck that night, there was no friend."

"What?"

I laugh and tell her the story of ending up behind the bar and in the truck. How the truck brought me to the ranch and how Blaze found me in the barn and everything that's happened since. How his whole family took me in and everything they did for me.

"Wow, girl, hold on to that guy. He's a good one."

"I know he is. When's the next time you're coming through Rock Springs?"

"Next week, actually."

"I'd love for you to have dinner with us and meet everyone."

"A real home-cooked meal? I can't say no to that! I can give you a call when I know my route better."

"Yes, please!"

"Okay, Riley. You take care and call or text more often. I like hearing from you. Not many girls to chat with on the road."

I laugh. "I promise."

We hang up, and I save her number in my phone and head downstairs to find Megan and Helen.

We share a late brunch and relax watching TV all afternoon. Helen gets up to make dinner, and Megan asks if she can paint my nails. I guess she wanted to try out a new brand before adding it to the shop.

We sit and talk about the shop, some of the town gossip, and a few crazy hairstyles she was asked for this week.

We all sit for dinner, and it just feels right, like family. It's a peace I haven't felt in years, since my parents died. Everyone talks and laughs. Even when they're joking on each other, you can see the love in their eyes.

"How is Sage?" I ask.

"Oh, she's a spitfire. Looks like she's coming home tomorrow. Colt is there taking care of her. He hasn't left her side," Helen says.

I can't help but smile at that. After dinner, Blaze asks me if I'll take a walk with him back to the house since it's ready, and I agree.

"I'm glad Sage is doing well."

"Yeah, she has been through worse, but it doesn't make it any easier." He slips his hand into mine.

I nod. We walk and talk a bit about the ranch and me starting school. I love how Blaze is so excited for me, sometimes more than I am.

"I'm nervous. I wasn't that great in high school. Granted, I didn't have a lot of support, but I'm still scared."

"We'll be here for you. If you need help, you can ask any one of us. We all did classes online." He squeezes my hand. "Sage can help with anything horse related. I can help with anything business related, and Colt and Mac are great around the ranch. You got this."

His faith in me warms my heart; knowing I have a support system calms my nerves.

"Mind if we stop by the barn? I got something I'd like to show you." He tilts his head toward the barn.

I nod. "That's fine."

We head over, and it's dark.

"Here, wait here. Let me get the lights." Blaze places me in the center of the main aisle.

I hear him shuffle over. When he flips the lights, I blink several times before I take in what I see in front of me. There are hundreds of twinkle lights strung up around the barn and hundreds of roses lining the aisle.

Just in front of me is a trailer that's now holding sheets of wood with the words 'Will You Marry Me' spelled out in white lights. My eyes water and when I turn around, Blaze is on one knee.

He takes my hand. "Riley, the day I found you in this barn changed my life. I'd never felt such possessiveness as I did then. My need to take care of you overwhelmed me. Watching you and seeing how strong you are, made me like you. Watching you get along with my family and fit in on the ranch like you've been here your whole life made me fall in love with you. I want to run this ranch with you by my side. I want to raise our kids here, raise them to love this land. I want to fall into bed every night with you in my arms. I love you, Riley. Will you do me the honor of being my wife?"

My eyes tear up, and there's a lump in my throat, so all I can do is nod.

"I need your words, baby."

I fall to my knees. "Yes! A thousand times yes!" I cry out and wrap my arms around him, and my lips find his.

The night I stumbled into this barn, I never thought my life would lead here. I was focused on surviving one day at a time. I now have the family I always wanted, the love of my life, and a place to call home. Most of all, I feel truly safe for the first time in my life. All because a trucker named Lilly took a chance on me and helped me when I had no one else in the world to do so.

Epilogue

Colt

No matter where my day started, I never thought I'd be riding in the back of an ambulance today. Riley is safe and we can all be happy about that. Sage kept her safe like she has done for several of us over the years. But once again, she is the one who got hurt.

Holding her hand in the back of this ambulance only solidifies what I already knew. I'm going to fight for us. I'm going to make her mine for good. Watching Blaze with Riley and how happy they are, I knew I wanted the same thing. I know Sage does too. Why else go on that date with Brice?

I will be the one to give her that life. She just needs to hang on. Before we even made it off the ranch, she passed out. The EMTs think it's her body's response to pain since her vitals are stable. I'm watching the heart monitor to make sure her heart keeps beating. Just keep her alive because I can't live without her. It was hard enough not to call her mine, but at least she was there on the ranch every day.

When we get to the hospital, the flurry of activity starts. But I refuse to leave her side even as they assess her injuries. Then one of the nurses who was here last time we were in this exact situation steps in. "Oh, honey, you two really need to stay out of trouble." She shakes her head ruefully.

Muttering, I say, "I'm trying, but she's just stubborn." Then I stand back letting the doctors do their job.

"I think she lost too much blood, and the pain is what caused her to pass out, the doctor confirms. "She hit her head?"

"I think so. She was on a hard floor."

"Ok, we'll give her some medication to keep her out while we do the tests and make sure there is no internal bleeding. Then we'll get her stitched up. Though we'll have to keep her for a day or two until she wakes up and we can make sure there is no head injury. Also, we'll need to make sure her blood count goes back up."

I nod, taking it all in. We aren't out of the woods yet, but Lord, if you will just watch over her this last time and bring her back to me, and make her okay, I swear I'll protect her better. I will go to church with her every Sunday and be the man she needs.

When they take her back for some tests, I head out to the waiting room to let the family know what's going on and see how Riley is.

Mom gives me this look and I wonder if she knows there is something more between Sage and me. We always kept it a secret from everyone. Mostly because we were living in the same house, and I know Mom and Dad wouldn't have liked it. But now there really isn't a reason.

"Well, boy, don't keep us waiting," Mom says almost the same way my birth mother always did which makes me realize I've just been standing there.

"She passed out in the ambulance. They think from the pain, but she's lost a lot of blood too. Her vitals are good. While they run some tests to check for internal injuries, they're going to keep her under. They stitched up the cut. Once she wakes up, they want to keep her for a few days. They'll be monitoring to make sure there's no head injury and see how she does. She is on the verge of needing a blood transfusion, but they're not sure yet. Since her vitals are okay, they're holding off."

That's when Blaze walks up beside me with Riley pressed to his side.

"You hear all that?" I ask, not really in the mood to repeat it.

"Yeah," he says.

"How Riley?" Mom asks.

"Blaze insisted Riley be checked over as well." Megan fills me in from beside me.

"She's fine. A few cuts and scrapes and she'll be sore in the morning. Listen, I was thinking we need to get that window fixed and..."

"We will handle it, son. Let's wait and see how Sage is," Dad says.

"Tim, you know he hates waiting, and he wants to do something," Mom says.

"I'll head back and text when I know more," I say.

I love my family, but with seven of them in the small waiting room, it can be a bit much. So, I wait in the room for news on Sage.

A nurse peeks her head in.

"Hey, they are moving her to her own room on the third floor. If you want to come with me, you can be there when she gets back from the tests."

"Thanks."

I follow her and thankfully it looks like Sage has her own room. Then I shoot a text to the family with the room number.

Now I need a plan. How do I win this girl back? I know she thinks I'm a playboy. I let her think it because I was so mad at the way she left. But now that's going to work against me. How do you convince someone the rumors aren't true?

I know we'll have lots of time for talking coming up, but it can't hurt to have a plan, right? When we get home, I'm going to take care of her just like I did after everything that happened with Mac's dad.

When they finally wheel her into the room and get her situated, she looks much better. It helps that she's now out of her bloody clothes. Even so, she looks so damn beautiful with the kind of beauty she doesn't even know she has. One look at her can make my heart skip a beat.

For the next several hours, I am planning how I will make her mine. Starting with attending church with her and Mom. That will give me extra time with her each week. Every chance I get, I'll be there at her house. No more avoiding her. I'll help with dinner and remind her how good we are together.

Because we are good together. We have always been better together than apart. That hasn't changed. I'm lost in date planning when the most beautiful sound in the world fills the room.

"Colt?"

· · · · ●·●·● ● · ·

Want Sage and Colt's Story? Get it in book 2 in the Rock Springs Texas series **The Cowboy and His Best Friend.**

· · · · ●·●·● ● · ·

Want more of Riley and Blaze? Find out the big news they have at their wedding and a super hot a steamy night after!
Join my newsletter to get 2 bonus epilogues.
https://www.kacirose.com/RunawayBonus
Already a subscriber? Check the bottom of my emails for details to get all the bonus content!

Connect with Kaci M. Rose

Kaci M. Rose writes steamy small town cowboys. She also writes under Kaci Rose and there she writes wounded military heroes, giant mountain men, sexy rock stars, and even more there. Connect with her below!

Website
Facebook
Kaci Rose Reader's Facebook Group
Goodreads
Book Bub
Join Kaci M. Rose's VIP List (Newsletter)

More Books by Kaci M. Rose

Rock Springs Texas Series

The Cowboy and His Runaway – Blaze and Riley

The Cowboy and His Best Friend – Sage and Colt

The Cowboy and His Obsession – Megan and Hunter

The Cowboy and His Sweetheart – Jason and Ella

The Cowboy and His Secret – Mac and Sarah

Rock Springs Weddings Novella

Rock Springs Box Set 1-5 + Bonus Content

Cowboys of Rock Springs

The Cowboy and His Mistletoe Kiss – Lilly and Mike

The Cowboy and His Valentine – Maggie and Nick

The Cowboy and His Vegas Wedding –
Royce and Anna
The Cowboy and His Angel – Abby and
Greg
The Cowboy and His Christmas Rockstar –
Savannah and Ford
The Cowboy and His Billionaire – Brice and
Kayla

About Kaci M Rose

Kaci M Rose writes cowboy, hot and steamy cowboys set in all town anywhere you can find a cowboy.

She enjoys horseback riding and attending a rodeo where is always looking for inspiration.

Kaci grew on a small farm/ranch in Florida where they raised cattle and an orange grove. She learned to ride a four-wheeler instead of a bike (and to this day still can't ride a bike) and was driving a tractor before she could drive a car.

Kaci prefers the country to the city to this day and is working to buy her own slice of land in the next year or two!
Kaci M Rose is the Cowboy Romance alter ego of Author Kaci Rose.

See all of Kaci Rose's Books here.

Please Leave a Review!

I love to hear from my readers! Please **head over to your favorite store and leave a review** of what you thought of this book!

Made in the USA
Monee, IL
12 March 2024

54369515R00154